To Beth N

My heartfelt thanks for
in reviewing my early drafts of
first novel - it is both valued and
appreciated.
thanks so much. -

Jd Bua (Voyles)

Huntington Creek Press
P. O. Box 22007
Chattanooga, TN 37422

Copyright 2020 by
Huntington Creek Press

ISBN: 9798665030067
Library of Congress Control Number: 2020936638

Dilemma: Choosing between two unfavorable alternatives.

My dilemma was picking which of the two men standing before me I must shoot first.

The one on the left, tall, hawk-faced with a scar down his left cheek and a tattoo up his neck, or the thick man on the right, his eyes squinted into narrow slits. Both held drawn pistols at their side.

My decision was complicated by the Glock 43 in my grip was still inside my jacket pocket. The round chambered would fire—and the slide would cycle back, trying to flick out the empty brass, but the folds of the pocket would push the brass back into the chamber as the slide slammed forward, tangling with the new round attempting to feed into the empty barrel. A jam.

A jam that could only be cleared by withdrawing the pistol and jacking the slide, hopefully allowing gravity to clear the chamber and dropping the empty brass and the live round now jammed to the pavement, allowing a new live round to feed and be ready for the second shot. It takes time. Too much time.

During that time either of the men I did not shoot would have time, maybe a lifetime, to raise the pistol in his hand at his side and fire before I could clear my weapon. At

10-feet he could not miss. Who would be the slower to react?

A dilemma whose decision time was down to milliseconds. I locked eyes and caught one man's eyes widen—the choice made. The only sound I could hear was my heart. Kawhump. And it began, slower than slow motion. I saw his eyes widen more and heard another heartbeat. Kawhump.

This was nothing I had envisioned in my worst nightmare, but here it was. I am not sure I heard my shot, but as my small cylinder of jacketed lead bore through my jacket and onward to its intended target, before I knew if my gambit was even half effective, the rush of events that had brought me to this point flashed through my mind like an hour long movie crammed into a half-second, before I heard my next heartbeat, the reason I was here was a single name whispering in neon. Carolyn.

Chapter 2

Most things that take me out of my routine of facing a computer screen listing desired collectibles for sale to an internet audience of collectors and dealers are usually phone calls. Often a friend or a referral to some old timer with a hoard of things collected over a lifetime and he now is old, the kids have no interest, spending all their extra cash on this week's new smartphone, and a friend of a friend told him I was the person to contact. I have the buyers, and I can sell it for him. My commission is how I make my living.

Few of these collectors in my market use a cell phone for anything except a phone conversation. As one old timer told me, "I have no need for a smartphone. I'm smart enough to dial a number, that's all I need a phone for."

This time was not a phone call but a text message. Few text message leads turn into anything for me. The text rather than the call indicates younger owners who are tech-savvy themselves with no need of the efforts and expertise of an online dealer.

However, I did not ignore the text, for there are rare times when the text is from the offspring of an old customer, who is now giving their Dad or Grandad a hand in the liquidation of the collection.

This text was one of those times. I almost ignored it. My cell was on the edge of my desk under a paperback and reaching for it brought that shot of pain in my back. L4 and L5 was how the chiropractor described it. So far, he had been accurate in the description but not so accurate in a successful treatment.

My lack of organization in my cluttered office had me shuffling through my stacks for a provenance statement on a Revolutionary War era tomahawk. It was sold if I could come up with the paperwork that I knew was here somewhere. Finding that paper was more important than a long-shot lead via a text message, but business was slow, I had already received a call concerning an overdue doctor's bill that the insurance had not paid, and a potential lead is a potential lead.

The text was simple, "Was given your name by Bob Ellridge (the name was not familiar) who said you could help me with a problem. Please let me know when you can be in the Los Angeles area. Thanks. Carolyn."

It was a vague text, and presumptive that I would spend the time to go across the country on spec, but there was the one thing that aroused my curiosity and prompted a quick call. I have an attraction (my friends call it an affliction) for anyone named Carolyn.

My first Carolyn, I call her Carolyn 1 in retrospect, was beautiful—at least as beautiful as a 13-year-old girl can be to a 12-year-old boy like I was. Her cousin was a friend, and together the three of us would ride bicycles every afternoon down the few designated bike paths along the old abandoned railroad tracks in our small Carolina mountain town, snaking through the woods near the black rusted trestle along Shaker Creek, and sometimes with our bikes in a jumbled pile we would sit on the big flat rock at the Stratton meadow and talk.

I soaked in her every word, I relived them in my sleep at night. I dreamed of her wide blue eyes with her direct stare. I was smitten.

We talked, I flirted, and she ignored me, which in turn made me flirt more, which blossomed into love in my mind. I received no encouragement to fuel my obsession, but it was there just the same, making me more determined to win her affection and attention. Even now I'm not sure if it was love or merely obsession, but it was something that touched my very soul.

Carolyn I's father took a better job as a factory manager producing fancy door hinges a few cities away less than a year after we began our daily rides, and now without our bike rides in common, there was no contact. I did obtain her address from her cousin, but never worked up the courage to write—and through that cousin, I was receiving updates on her from time to time. I never lost my obsession.

Through her cousin, I learned a few years later that she had given herself to the local bad boy in Pelham, Alabama, who in turn soon thereafter had taken his Honda head-on into a city garbage truck.

At 15 years of age in that part of the world, despite laws to the contrary, sex occurred. Some would be heartbroken that the love of their life, their three-year infatuation had given herself to someone other than me. I did wish that it could have been me, not just to fulfill my teenage lust but to, no matter what, always be remembered as her first. Only one person could be first—but it had not been me.

My pragmatic side consoled me with the suspicion that if I ever did manage to get close to her again, the odds of consummating my yearning sexual desire with my dream girl was now greatly increased, with the virginity barrier down. Looking back, I call that 15-year-old reasoning, encouraged by teenage longings that were screaming inside my head that it was time I got laid for the first time.

I didn't realize things like that usually come to fruition at that age by luck.

Chapter 3

I have been lucky a few times in my life. As a kid at the county fair, I did win a bingo prize, and along with my Mom and Dad, I was led into the center area where the prizes were stacked and walked round and round the stack looking for a toy, of which there were none. Finally, my exasperated Dad said, "We have to go, it is time to pick." Still looking for my toy I didn't answer. That was how my first lucky prize ended up being a plastic salad bowl with a large plastic fork and spoon.

Sometimes when you go a long time with no good luck, it seems to dump itself on your like a bucket of water, giving you a miracle. I am a believer in miracles. I have seen them happen, got close on others.

Custer had luck. They wrote articles in the Civil War newspapers of George Armstrong Custer leading charges from the front and surviving the war with mere scratches. George Armstrong himself called it the "Custer luck."

In the Plains Wars whenever he formed his 7th Cavalry into an attack formation, the Indians would break and flee. Custer's luck, until that one day on the Little Bighorn when he used up all his luck and the reaper came to collect the bill.

***

No one could say I had used up my luck on that day in that Texas parking garage. I can attest that on at least one occasion in history, a 9 mm Glock 43 fired from within a pocket successfully ejected the spent round and threw another up the spout in a single cycle of the bolt. And while luck and miracles were flowing, there is no further explanation other than luck that the first offhand shot from the pocket, intended to hit chest high, instead struck the hawk-faced man a half inch over his right eye and blew the top half of his head away. The time from when I first faced off with my two assailants was four heartbeats. Now came the fifth ka-whump of my pulse of blood through my body.

I wasn't certain the second round had chambered tight, but I did hear the satisfying click of the bolt slamming home. It was my only play left as I turned to the second man, his gun rising, his companion's body still in the process of yielding to the earth's pull. Again, another heartbeat, the hawk-faced man collapsed into a lifeless heap where an instant before a living breathing human had stood. Half of my problem was over.

As I pulled the trigger again, my body turned toward the second man, the pistol still in my pocket. I was rewarded with the sound of the pistol firing, and a further replay echoed in my mind of the single name that had brought me here. Carolyn.

#

Chapter 4

It is hard to explain my Carolyn factor, and Carolyn II or Carolyn III without finishing my exploits with Carolyn I.

Carolyn I returned for a single visit late in my 15th year, bloomed into the beautiful woman I envisioned she would become when I drooled after her three years earlier.

Nothing of my infatuation had lessened. Once I saw her again, it intensified. I was in love—and lust.

Her hair was now a short brown that framed her model face, her eyes bluer, more captivating, still wide and direct and her smile melted me. Her family had come back to finalize the sale of their property in Huntington. She had come along. I fantasized she had come to see me.

This time was different. Carolyn I paid attention to my flirting and flirted back. It was ecstasy. Their visit coincided with the Oconoluftee County day-long field day/annual fair event that started mid-morning and continued with live music late into the night. It was easy enough to give her a call and find out when she was going. I was there when she arrived.

Together Carolyn and I walked the twisting paths of the park. I reached for her hand and she took it, a touch that flashed sparks up my arm. She was holding my hand. My Carolyn was holding hands with me. I was not going to let her go, ever. We continued, she walked, I floated, holding hands, our bodies connected and touching as I had dreamed. Each intake of breath bore a whiff of her perfume. I soaked in every hint of a smile, each raised eyebrow or widening of those deep blue eyes. We talked of music, and old bike rides and caught up on her life till now. She laughed at the right times, snickered at the innuendo remarks, and reached into my soul and locked on to my heart.

There was one complication, in the form of a cute blonde named Lucinda with long straight hair that fell almost to her waist. A year younger, the acclaimed beauty of her class, and the one person to which I was almost attached. She had told one of her friends she thought I was cute. I thought she looked pretty good, and told my friend, so working like seconds in a duel, my friend arranged a bump-into for Lucinda and myself via her friend, and we were soon walking together during lunch period, exhibiting to the student body that we were becoming "a thing."

The next natural step was to ask her to go steady, and in the evolution of things, tonight looked to be the night that should occur. But that was before Carolyn dropped back into my life like one of those safes falling on the coyote in one of those Roadrunner cartoons.

Lucinda was to arrive at 6 p.m. after her Mother got off work at the Burger King. Time was closing in on me.

During my heart opening admission of my long unrequited love for Carolyn, to her question, "Are you seeing anyone right now," I told the truth.

"What does she look like?" Carolyn asked. "I want to see if I have anything to worry about." I showed Carolyn the picture of Lucinda in my wallet. "Wow, maybe I do," Carolyn said, "She's pretty." I took that as she was worried about competition for my attention. I was still flying. It was 5:45. Who was Lucinda? I had my Carolyn.

"She's not you," I said. The answer seemed to satisfy her, at least until our paths crossed those of three lanky upperclassmen, one who recognized her from years before and called to her. "Hey there". Gerald moved between us.

"I remember you," he said. "Carolyn, wasn't it?"

I knew this to be trouble. While his two cronies were simply assholes, Gerald was much worse, a full-blown bully and asshole. I hated him. He felt the same about me, I knew.

Worse, Gerald was big, tough, and had made it his personal goal to make my life as miserable as possible. He was very good at it. What I foresaw in an instant was soon he would be figuring out a way to start some crap with me that would end with my carrying away bruises and insults to my ego and well-being. Even worse it would be in front of my Carolyn.

Carolyn sized the situation up quickly and looked over at me. "You have an obligation at six, you go on, I understand. I'll see you tomorrow."

Another thing I hated about Gerald was girls fell all over him. "He's so cute," was the common squeal. I hated him even worse now when I saw how Carolyn was looking at him, that same attentive look that had been uniquely mine minutes before.

"But..." I stammered to Carolyn. I would like to think that my dear Carolyn recognized I was about to receive a genuine beating and was bailing me out of the situation, but as events would play out, the subject of my many hours of desire and lust for three years was bailing on me, my love who was gripping my heart and tiptoeing toward bliss was blowing me off.

"Tomorrow," she smiled, and I melted and faded, my heart on the ground underneath her feet.

One saving grace was the resilience of a 15-year-old hormone enraged boy. At least I did have somewhere else to go where another pretty girl waited.

Chapter 5

My consolation prize of the evening, Lucinda, knew nothing of my Carolyn infatuation.

She was waiting at the park entrance as promised. With my mind jumbled from what happened minutes before and trying not to let it show, like most of the other dating couples we began our own walk down the park paths I had trod earlier, my mind confused, wanting both girls. Lucinda was here. Carolyn was more in my heart though, so far away from me, all the rejection of those old days—and no acceptance until now, only to end so bad tonight. But she had said, "tomorrow." I still had a chance.

Carolyn and Lucinda. It was the most delightful problem imaginable—and it was twisting me into knots.

I made it a point to go in the opposite direction in which Carolyn and I had been walking. In a dark twist of the path, my blonde came into my arms for a quick five-minute make-out session before the crunch of approaching feet on the gravel path forced us onward.

This was our first opportunity to be alone and intimate. The first kiss on new lips is always memorable.

We meandered through the winding paths for the better part of an hour, seeking the dark corners, and I pressed her warm nubile body against mine as our lips and tongues explored each other with the newness that only a 15-year-old could enjoy. I was a boy thinking I was a man, being bold for the first time. Prior to tonight, everything had been quick kissing. This was hot making out.

The third time we stopped to kiss my hand moved forward, sliding carefully and slowly up her side and higher, moving over the soft mound of her bra clad breast. She did not object. When she felt my touch instead of shoving my hand away, or a soft "no", she pulled me tighter.

Oh my God, I was touching my first female breast. Softness beyond comprehension, thrill beyond imagination, my first time to first base. Again, an interruption from feet on gravel coming up the path, forcing me to cease my fondling, but no one could ever take away from me the memory or the realization of that step toward manhood, or my affection for the lovely cute blonde that let it happen.

Again, we stopped to embrace, and again the crunching of feet on gravel interrupted our idyll. We began walking again, my arm around her waist for a while before realizing it was easier to walk by holding hands.

We eventually came to be on the path that led by the parking lot. The first line of cars was facing the elevated path, and I recognized Gerald's red pick-up in that line, half-hidden from the streetlights by the shade of a massive live oak.

Lucinda and I passed in front of his truck, holding hands, Lucinda on my left and the parking lot on my right. I caught movement in the cab of the red truck. By instinct, I turned to glance and caught someone on the passenger side of the truck. The movement clear in that dim light was that of a female moving over the person's lap to straddle them. Even in that dimness, I could see the female's unclothed back and the brown bob of hair. It was Carolyn, in Gerald's truck, with her top off.

The only sound was our feet crunching in the gravel on the path, but deep inside there was another sound, that of my heart ripping to shreds.

I took Lucinda's hand and picked up our pace, distancing from the shock of what I had seen.

I would like to say the rest of the night made up for the painful scene and Lucinda rescued me from my misery.

But it didn't happen. There was no rescue from my heartbreak.

Reality was Lucinda's Mom waiting to take her home, not too pleased she was walking in public holding hands with a boy, and she hustled her daughter into their van and I watched them drive away, the smell of Lucinda's perfume still on my clothes, the taste of her bubblegum flavored lipstick still on lips and an aching pain for Carolyn in my heart that never went away.

A wise person would have said that was the end with Carolyn I, but not to a stubborn 15-year-old grasping at straws. To paraphrase an adage about the bird in the hand is worth two in the bush, "a breast in the hand..." But then there was what Carolyn I had promised, "tomorrow", and despite what I had seen the night before I clung to that forlorn hope as I lay awake that night anticipating the coming day—and Carolyn.

It was lunchtime before my household chores were done and I showered, polished my shoes, checked myself in the mirror and combed my hair just right, even splashing a bit of the old man's aftershave although my need for aftershave was four years in the future.

My bike was still my primary mode of transportation, and I set out down the sidewalk toward Carolyn's grandmother's place, careful to not pedal so fast as to work up a sweat.

Carolyn I's grandmother's house had a detached garage with a huge evergreen that brushed the outside edge of the building, and as I approached, I saw a form almost hidden by the evergreen. In the gap, I made out two people locked in a passionate kiss, Gerald and Carolyn. I coasted on by without pedaling or slowing. I never saw Carolyn I again.

I would think about her over the years, whenever I would hear that old Beach Boy's song, "Caroline No", but I would alter the lyric as I sang along, "Oh Carolyn No."

Chapter 6

It is better to be lucky than good, although getting a second shot toward my second assailant surely consumed most of what luck that had come my way. It struck the thick older man in the right shoulder, his gun arm. The impact spun him half around and by reflex, he squeezed off a round into the concrete before losing his grip and the pistol went flying. My heartbeats roared in my ears like a startled pheasant struggling airborne.

I had pulled the Glock from my pocket. The ejection of the second round had jammed the action. I tugged back on the slide, turning the pistol to its side and shaking as I did, the welcome sound of brass falling to the pavement reaching my ears and releasing the slide it sprang forward and seated the next round.

The wounded man opposite me was in a squat, his left-hand clawing at an exposed ankle holster holding a snub nose .38. It was set up for a right-hand draw, forcing him to reach around his leg, costing him time—time that he did not have.

I screamed, "No. Stop. Freeze." He didn't, and I did a tap-tap with two rounds to the body mass. His body rolled back and didn't move. The pouring blood told me he was not wearing body armor.

My mind numb, I picked up the brass and my unfired round from the parking deck floor and forced myself to walk away in a steady casual pace, despite my trembling. I kept listening for sirens but heard none as I rode the elevator to the basement, walked through the service area into an isolated alley littered with broken whiskey bottles and smelling like piss where I braced myself against a wall and vomited. Again, that single name flashed through my mind and what fates had brought me here. One name, Carolyn.

Chapter 7

Carolyn II was different, a transfer, who happened to be assigned the seat in front of me in Mrs. Tatum's Info Technology class my Senior year. She was chatty, and she and I had opportunity to chat as Mrs. Tatum's class was the first one following lunch and Mrs. Tatum was talkative in her own right—and often extended her conversations in the teacher's lounge.

I had no objection—as it seemed Carolyn II and I would finish lunch quicker than most and thus have more conversation time during lunch period and running into Mrs. Tatum's delayed start to the IT class. I did not know if she finished quick intentionally to be in class earlier with me, but I know I did.

The additional factor that forced me to rush through my lunch and rush to the computing classroom for my chat session with a new Carolyn, this Carolyn was pretty—very pretty, with long legs, long straight blonde hair, and a propensity for tight ribbed tank tops in pastel colors.

Every guy in school wanted her—but I was the only one to whom she paid any attention. She had a friendly personality the other girls called "sweet" and I summed up personally as captivating—and captivate me she did. Carolyn II captivated all my attention and my desire.

Her parents were fundamental Christians who restricted her dating—at least that was the excuse she used the first three times she turned me down when I asked for a date. Never a no, but just enough encouragement to keep me hanging on, and I desperately clung to that hope.

When the annual PTA carnival arrived, the fund-raising event that celebrated the end of the school year, each class selected candidates to run for King and Queen of the carnival. When Carolyn II was nominated and selected as Queen candidate, it was time to select the class candidate for King. My best friend Kyle nominated me, and I was selected.

This campaign meant Carolyn II and I worked together on the fundraising, spent more hours together, and on the announcement night with me in a new suit and she in a prom dress, together arm and arm we wandered through the crowd playing the teacher-managed sideshow games with a bucket soliciting last-minute donations, as was the custom for all the candidates. The winner was selected by whoever raised the most money for the PTA and be named King and Queen of the Carnival.

The witching hour of 10 arrived, the cash was counted, and the announcement made. We lost. All our work, the car washes, the bake sales, the solicitations, all was for a second-place finish. Second always sucks, then and now.

I hugged her in consolation; we could not hide our disappointment. Friends gave us a wide berth as we stood together in a quiet corner in the hall. We were not talking, but I felt there was something transpiring between us in our shared misery.

As the event broke up Carolyn II moved toward her family and toward the exit. In a moment of inspiration, I followed with the idea of me presenting myself in front of her parents. At the least, I envisioned asking if I could drive her home and we could continue to console each other on our defeat (complete with my plans to take the short cut on the gravel road to their house which would give me at least five minutes of make-out time).

I pushed through the crowd toward her and the flow of people stopped to let cars pass on the street between the venue and the parking lot. I was twenty feet away when I saw a blue Chevy Camaro pull up with two husky guys with no necks that I recognized as football standouts from our rival high school.

One guy got out, flipped the front seat forward and climbed into the back. In front of my eyes, Carolyn climbed into the back beside him, in front of her parents. She pulled the front of the seat back and saw me, with no recognition from her that I was anyone other than another face in the crowd. I was a part of the wall.

Her best friend Becky took the seat beside the driver. The door shut, and they pulled away. My weeping heart went with her. We shared no classes after that.

Chapter 8

Daniel Bays runs a cutlery shop an upscale LA mall, and we were friends from the first time our paths crossed in the buying and selling of collectibles with sharp edges. I called him.

"You know anyone named Bob Ellridge?"

"Oh yeah, he came into the shop a few days ago, said he was looking for someone to sell a nice piece of cutlery for a friend. He said you had done something for him in the past, but he had lost your number. He knew we were friends. I gave it to him."

I was less apprehensive about taking a trip to the west coast. It would be a good excuse to see my old friend Daniel and his family either way.

I had texted Carolyn back, telling her I was interested in seeing how I could help her situation, I ended with a "Who are you? I do not have the last name."

Again, a text. Her name was Carolyn McMasters, and the text was terse, "You have a reservation at the Marriott on Century Boulevard beside LAX. The Hertz desk downstairs will have a car reserved in your name. My address will be with the reservation form. Text once you land or if you have any problems. If we cannot come to terms, I will reimburse your travel expenses."

Flights are plentiful to Los Angeles, and a call confirmed I did have a ticket and reservations. The day following the text I was in a crowded Delta cabin next to an obese woman in a dirty gray tank top, trying my best to zone out with my Bose headphones and music from my phone. It did not work well.

It was dark when I arrived and despite the buzz of the sports bar in the lobby, I opted for an elevator ride to the 8th floor, a long hot shower, and bed.

I waited for the messy tangle of LA traffic to lighten, and at 10 the next morning I headed North up the 405 to Santa Barbara, weaving through the treeless hills and then up the coast.

The large brass elephant head door knocker on the massive wood door was answered by a casually dressed Latina woman who led me to a large room with a huge glass wall overlooking the Pacific..

The woman I was to meet was staring out at the water, her back to me. If the long dusty brown hair and tight butt in those beige pants was any indication of what the front side of this Carolyn looked like, she was breathtaking. As she turned, even with those seconds of mental prep, I still gave a small gasp when she faced me.

Breathtaking was an understatement. She looked better from the front than she did from behind. Long legs, high cheekbones, wide-set green eyes, full thick lips. I tried to think of an actress she might resemble but stopped somewhere between Charlize Theron and Cindy Crawford in her prime.

Her beige top matched the pants, clingy like metallic silk, open far enough to reveal a bit of cleavage, a hint of lace. Neat, clean, nothing out of place, the right earrings and necklace to accent perfectly. The way she carried herself told me she was acutely aware of her appearance—and the effect she had on men. I was no exception. She was gorgeous.

Carolyn McMasters waited before she spoke, observing my reaction, letting the impact of her beauty sink in, but her tone was aloof and all business, almost brusque.

My gut, the tiny bit of instinct that had saved me at times in the past was screaming, "Caution, Caution." Carolyns had too many times in my past proved trouble for me. Maybe it was no more than obsessive compulsion that had drawn me on this trip, but I had satisfied my curiosity about what this Carolyn looked like. She reaffirmed my theory there are few ugly women named Carolyn.

The woman treated my reaction nonplussed. She was used to male reactions like mine. Any woman that looked like her had to. She didn't walk to me, it was more like a glide, her back ramrod straight and looking straight into my face.

There was something else, a coldness, a wall. I could almost feel the cool chill of her to the point of disdain that she was forced to deal with someone like me. I suspect my thick Southern accent would not help things.

"Mr. Kugar," she said flatly, extending her hand. "So glad you could make it. I'm Carolyn McMasters." I saw no emotion, no smile nor even a hint of a smile.

"Pleased to meet you," I said. She went through the quick formalities of asking if I would like coffee or a drink. I settled on coffee. "Too early for me to start drinking."

"Yes, only a reprobate would drink before noon," she said, turning to the Latina. "Rosa, would you bring me a mimosa, please. We'll be on the deck. Come along Mr. Kugar." I followed, her high heels clicking on the slate floor.

"You can call me Max," I said. "Mr. Kugar is far too formal for someone like me. Mr. Kugar is my late father."

"I thought all you Southern boys liked to use 'Mr.' and 'Sir' and open doors."

"We try as much as we are allowed," I said reaching for the door to open it only to see her step-in in front of me and open the door herself.

"Well, we are in California, Max. May as well act like it."

We took a seat at a round white metal table with striped plush cushions in the chairs, the coffee and her drink arriving instantaneously. The coffee was in a French press, and Rosa poured my cup at the table. A soft sea breeze rattled the matching striped umbrella over our head.

"You said I had something you thought I could help you with?"

"Yes. I think your background may be just what I need." I must have looked puzzled. "I did check you out first, you know. Bob Ellridge suggested you."

"I'm not sure I know him."

"He certainly knows you. You sold some things for his father-in-law, discretely, he said."

I backpedaled through my mind, "Bob", "California". It took a minute. "Speria? He is the son-in-law of Edgar Speria?" I asked.

"Yes, his father in law is Edgar Speria. I met Mr. Speria at a party of Bob's once."

I had met with Speria's son-in-law Bob on that one, although my meeting with him had been brief and I wasn't sure I had caught his last name. Once alone with Speria, he and I had concluded our business alone and face to face.

Discretion was indeed required. Speria had accumulated one of the largest collections of fine elephant ivory handmade knives in the world, carved ivory Randall knives by Tom Leschorn, scrimshawed ivory handled knives by Bob Engnath and even a dozen ivory knives by Buster Warenski, Bob Loveless, and Jess Horn that he had commissioned. What made them even more unique was

Speria, a serious art buyer as well, commissioned a few of the leading painters in the art world to scrim the ivory handles of his knives.

There were two reasons we had to be low key on the sale. One was many of the artists had required in their contract that their names never be associated with the media of elephant ivory. Each of them had succumbed to the commission check, and as their reputations had risen in the art world, the prices of any examples of their work rose as well, giving Speria a sizable return on investment—had he been able to legally auction them.

Which brought us to the second more important reason I was contacted. The U. S. Fish & Wildlife Service in response to political pressure from wildlife groups and the endorsement of the Obama administration enacted regulations that made it illegal to sell any knife with elephant ivory less than 100 years old.

"So, you have ivory handled knives?" I asked Carolyn. I had required secrecy in the Speria transaction and was not happy someone else now knew about it. Discretion went both ways.

"No," she said, sipping on her mimosa, her head down and peering at me over the top of her glass. "But something perhaps more delicate." Her soft features hardened, and her eyes became more intense as if x-raying my soul. She sat the glass down on the glass top table with a clink.

"Do you finish jobs you start?" she asked.

"I always have."

"Bob says you have no problems selling things through, let's say 'less than normal channels'?"

"Let's," I said. "It depends on the illegality of what I'm being asked to sell."

"Nothing illegal per se," Carolyn said, "But something of, maybe questionable provenance."

"I do not deal in fakes. Fraud is not my business. I could answer better if I knew what we were talking about."

Carolyn did not answer my question. "Do you hunt?" I thought that a strange question but answered.

"Yes, I do."

"Do you hunt because you like to kill things?" She asked, her head tilting.

"No. I hunt because I enjoy being outdoors, I do it as a tradition I guess, honoring my father who took me into the woods to learn about the outdoors the same way his father did him. It is not about the killing."

"You have killed?" Until I knew where this was going, I was not going to give anything away. Short concise answers would do.

"Animals, yes."

"Defenseless animals?" This was where I was afraid the conversation was heading, but sitting on a deck in Santa Barbara, California there were not a lot of other ways for the conversation to go, I suppose.

"Not always."

"So, you have hunted dangerous animals?" She still gave no indication why she was she was going with this questioning.

"I have. Bear."

"Any close calls?" Carolyn leaned over the table, closer.

"One in particular," I said.

"Tell me about it."

"We were dogging bear in the North Carolina mountains; I could hear something big rustling through the crisp dry leaves. A large black bear burst out of the laurel into the bare logging road and I only had time for a snapshot. Instead of running away up the mountain to safety, the bear turned toward me and charged. I didn't know he was charging at the time. According to most hunting books, a black bear does not charge, but this one, if it was fleeing, was wanting to flee right over the top of me. He had his ears back and was grunting a "woof, woof, woof" as he closed. I fired three more times and he kept coming. Later I would read that ears back and going "woof" is the ultimate sign of aggression in a black bear, so he was indeed charging. My last shot had him crumpling only feet away from me. I must have knocked my sights out of line was the only way I could explain the missed shots."

"You didn't try to run?"

"No time, no need. A bear can run 35 miles an hour. It was me or him face to face, I guess you'd say." I said.

"And?"

"I'm here."

"Did you mount the head? Make a rug?"

"No. I think the animal deserved more dignity than that. He died game, and my memory and a couple of photos with him is enough." Carolyn continued to stare at me without speaking. I wondered if I should shift in my seat to break her concentration, but I didn't—I stared back. Finally, she polished off the last of her mimosa and waved to Rosa for a refill.

"Bob was right, I think. You do seem steadfast for what I need. Yes, I think you will do."

"That still depends," I said. "I still do not know what you want me to do. I do not automatically take a job."

Carolyn excused herself for a second while I enjoyed the million-dollar view of the vast Pacific, only the roofs of a few beach houses down below us evidence that it was any different from when the first Spanish explorers had seen it.

I heard the click of her heels and the whiff of perfume before she came into view. I turned toward her. She returned with a large brown envelope. "I keep this in the safe." She made no move to open the envelope.

"I have a question," I asked.

"Yes."

"Why did you want to know if I hunted?"

"Oh nothing," she said, looking out at the ocean again, as if she was remembering something, and looked back at me, her voice softening from the stiff snappiness. "OK, my grandfather. He said to never trust a man who didn't hunt. Non-hunters do not get it about how things work in the world."

"Sounds like I'd like your grandfather," I said.

"Yeah, you probably would. He's dead now. And that is the reason you are here. Something I have inherited." She handed me the envelope. I didn't open it, waiting for her to invite me to delve into it first.

"Have you heard of the Honjo Masamune, Mr. Kugar?"

"Of course."

"What do you know of it?"

"It is one of the most famous swords ever made, supposedly made by Masamune, the most famous swordsmith in Japanese history. The sword is said to bear almost supernatural powers and convey the same to its owners.

"General Honjo Shigenaga, the owner for whom the sword is named, was attacked during a battle by a famous swordsman wielding the Honjo, with which the swordsman split Shigenaga's helmet. Swords are not supposed to split helmets, but this one did.

"Despite the blow, Shigenaga bested his opponent and took the Honjo as a prize. The blade reportedly still has some chips from that 13th-century battle. Toyotomi Hideyoshi owned it, and later it became the property of the Tokugawa shogunate, where it was passed down through the shoguns of the family from around 1600 until 1946. It was designated a Japanese National Treasure in 1939. Tokugawa Lemasa was the documented last owner."

"Very good. I'm impressed," she said.

"Nothing to be impressed about, anyone with an interest in swords knows that story. It's a legend."

"And what happened to this famous sword?"

"More legend. It disappeared at the end of World War II. All swords were required to be turned in as weapons of war and despite requesting the sword be exempted, that exemption was refused. Tokugawa Lemasa turned in the Honjo Masamune and 14 other swords at the Mejiro Police Department to the US government in January of 1946, per the regulations of the time. From there it disappeared and has not been seen since."

"That's my understanding too," she said. "Would you please examine the contents of the envelope.". She watched me as I read. It was notarized by an attorney with two witnesses and dated 2011.

> *To whom it may concern.*
>
> *I, Carlton McMasters, was attached to the Foreign Liquidations Commission of Army Forces, Western Pacific (AFWESPAC) from September 1945 until June 1946. During that time, I was charged with receiving swords turned in by the Japanese and collecting them for storage.*
>
> *In December of 1945, my friend Cody Biltmore told me there was a ruckus about a sword that the owner was resisting turning in, trying to go through official channels to have exempted, and that it was valuable and very important to some powerful Japanese.*

I had been fighting the damn Japs for two years, had good friends die beside me in the Philippines, and if I could take something that they wanted to keep—then count me in. I could no longer kill them, but any hurt I could inflict was fine with me.

Cody wanted my help getting that sword, so together we informed the police department in Mejiro, Japan that there was no exemption and the sword was to be turned in immediately, and it was. I took possession of the sword, but the police required a name for the receipt. Cody gave them his name but was laughing about it later because his name was written down as "Coldy Bimore."

I was to ship the sword home, and after he returned, we would sell the sword and split the money. I shipped the sword to my Mom and was discharged in San Francisco two months before Cody. We didn't decide where to meet while in Japan, but we had each other's address. I wrote to him while he was still in Japan, letting him know I was home, safe, and the thing we owned together was here safe too.

In his answer to my letter, he said he was questioned two times about receiving the sword, but he had denied any knowledge of it. He said he was worried because there were several Japanese men he thought were following him. That was the only letter I received from him.

I contacted his family at the address he had given me, and they told me he had been murdered in Japan in June of 1946, according to a telegram from the government. I was scared to let anyone know of my involvement and felt there were people desperate to find the sword and I suspect that was why he was killed.

"I put this to paper to set the record straight. I hope my taking the sword was not what caused the death of my friend, but for that reason, I have kept the sword in my *possession and told no one. If you are reading this, it is because I am dead. What ownership or claim I may have to the Honjo Masamune sword I bequeath to my children, Irena and Darby."*

I reread the letter and looked up into Carolyn's piercing stare. "Is this true?"

"Yes. I'm afraid it is."

"And your interest?"

"Darby was my mother. She passed away five years ago. My Aunt Irena never had children and died two years ago."

"You have the sword?"

"Yes, in a safe place."

"If you know all this, why are you talking to me?"

"I didn't know any of this until three months ago. Grandad never said anything about it to Mom as far as I know, but the lawyer contacted me after Grandad passed and said I had been left a few things from my Grandad's personal effects." She turned to me. "I want to sell the sword. I need someone to discreetly sell it for me."

***

Judging my history with women named Carolyn, I should have heard bells clanging inside my head screaming, "Carolyn Alert!" At the least, I need a buzzer app on my phone that vibrates each time the word "Carolyn" is mentioned around me. But they do not make such an app, so I was running on gut. Gut can fail you sometimes.

"OK, I'm interested," I said. "Do you have a price in mind?"

"It is a National Treasure," she said, "Surely it must be millions."

"It takes a buyer, and in your words, a 'discreet' buyer'."

"I know," Carolyn said, a half-smile lighting her face and changing her whole demeanor. It was an instant transformation that amazed me. And it was not a normal transition but one that had been practiced.

"Are you an actress?" I asked.

"I had some bit parts. Let me guess, you think you've seen me somewhere before?"

"No, not really," I said. "You are very pretty, we are in California, and you seem to have the talent to convey moods with your facial expressions. It adds up."

"Damn, you are pretty good," she smiled, for the first time exhibiting what I consider a natural expression. "I think all social interaction is acting, isn't it?"

"Maybe here," I said. "Sometimes it is refreshing to let go and be who we are without the facade or be at a place where few people have to put up facades."

"I don't know what that means anymore, or if such a place exists," Carolyn said, tossing it off. "But enough about me. About the sword. Are you willing to sell a Japanese National Treasure item right under their noses? And your terms?"

"30%. Plus $5000 up front for an advance on expenses. If I am unable to find a buyer, I keep the five grand for my trouble."

"That seems high," she said.

"OK, 35% and 10 grand," I said. "Now you can whittle me down to 30% and feel better. Being upfront saves time."

"What do I get for my 30%?" she asked. "And you did not answer my question. How do you feel about such a historical relic not being returned to Japan?"

"For my commission, you get my best effort, my discretion, and my acceptance of potential complications. As for the Japanese, I lost a great-uncle at Pearl Harbor, another on Saipan, and my great-aunt never recovered from it. They say my great grandmother died of a broken heart too because of the death of her son. I could care less about what the Japanese might want concerning their heritage. Their militaristic bushido code bullshit got members of my family killed.

"I know that is not a politically correct statement, but in my part of the world, we tend to have long memories and keep grudges. I have nothing against individual Japanese people, but I do not give a damn about their national heritage. There is a difference." I caught myself, realizing I had revealed more emotion than I like to exhibit to strangers.

"Ohhh," Carolyn said, "Like the Hatfields and McCoys."

"That occurred hundreds of miles away from where I was raised. That happened along the border between West Virginia and Kentucky. Different world." I paused, "I did have one ancestor who was a Hatfield, just for the record."

"What complications would you envision?" Carolyn asked.

"Someone in 1946 was serious enough about finding the sword to maybe have committed murder. I doubt for some people that would have changed. If the Japanese government got wind of this, I could see an international incident—and the sword confiscated for lack of a clear title of ownership and you get nothing."

"Nothing?"

"Nothing. And there is the provenance question."

"That part is easy," Carolyn said.

"How so?"

"I have detailed photographs of the temper line. I'm told it is like a fingerprint." She turned to leave the room and I followed, down a small hall into a sitting room with no windows and low lighting. A large easy chair was on one end, and a massive safe was partially open. She swung open the heavy door and withdrew another manila envelope. "You can keep these, I have copies," she said, replacing the document I had read, closed the door with a clunk and spinning the dial.

The walls were filled with photos, Carolyn at an award show in a low-cut evening gown, presenting the awards. Carolyn with a half dozen well-known actors and television celebrities, a couple of politicians, and a group photo of an older couple and a man who bore a strong resemblance to her, black hair long and pulled back in a ponytail. "My brother, Thomas," she said. "He is in Phoenix."

"Is he a part-owner of the sword?"

"No. My brother received some family acreage in New Mexico, I received all the contents of the homes Grandad owned. The sword was a part of that."

On the wall to the left of the safe was a large photo with a small light illuminating it, a silver oxide print. The photo weaved shadows of the nude human form, a partial view of high cheekbones and deep eyes, a bare back, the side of a breast, and long legs. It took a second before I recognized the model—Carolyn.

"Tonny Herbert," she said. "When a photographer of that stature wants to photograph you, one does not say 'no', and she poses as he directs. He calls this photograph

'Shadows and Light.' I wanted a classy nude while I was in my prime."

"It is beautiful," I said. "Beauty and eroticism and innocence in a single shot."

"That was what Tonny described, he was looking for in the photo when he was shooting me. You know something of photography?"

"I appreciate great photography," I said. "I've sold a few Ansel Adams photos in the past. A Man Ray or two also. This is lovely."

"Thank you," she almost smiled. Something about the way she said it annoyed me.

"I was talking about the photographer," I said. "Although you help make the photograph what it is."

"Help?" she said. "And you used the word "innocence" when you described it. Do you really see the innocence in that photo?"

"I do."

"You may not know as much about photography as you think, Mr. Kugar," Carolyn said, motioning toward the entrance to the room. "Please."

Back in the larger room, I opened the photos of the sword, clear and precise and well done. "You say you wanted discretion?" I said.

"Yes."

"Who took the photos? Photographers like to keep copies."

"I did. You don't hang around photographers without picking up a thing or two. At this moment the only people who know about the sword are you and I."

"The lawyer?"

"He didn't read the notarized letter; he only delivered the envelope. The sword was in a locked case. He has no idea of the case contents."

"And your brother?"

"The envelope was addressed to me. Mom's name had been struck through and replaced with mine. It was Grandad's handwriting, and he added my nickname."

"Nickname?"

"Yes, I had one. No, you are not allowed to know it. It was between Grandad and me."

"Fair enough," I said. "Do people in Japan have photos of the temper line of the Honjo?"

"That and very detailed drawings, some dating back many years and others as recent as 1939 with the declaration of the sword as a National Treasure. You will have no problem proving the authenticity of the sword," she said.

"Does your brother have a claim to the sword? Does he know about it?"

"I'll tell him when the time comes. I do not have to, but I will give him a share of the proceeds, if for nothing more to keep peace in the family. My brother can be a real ass."

Carolyn reached into a narrow table and opened the drawer, laying a pack of bills on the table. "Here's the advance," she said. "I anticipated that amount as your usual fee."

"You did check me out, didn't you?"

"I told you I did. I know you are not wealthy. You need this job Mr. Kugar. Another reason to retain you. I know you are hungry. I need someone hungry. Bob attested to your skills. I assume you will check me out as soon as you get to a computer. I would. Feel free, what you see is pretty well what you get."

In a better mood with a couple of drinks, and a woman in a more receptive mood my first comeback would have been, "I've been checking you out since I arrived," but I said nothing.

The aura she exuded was still cold indifference and dark. My sideways flirt would not have been appreciated. The thought of me getting what I was seeing from an aesthetic sense had a certain appeal, even though that had nothing to do with the context in which she said it. Emotionally, I sensed an emptiness. Again, I said nothing. This was business and she wasn't offering a come-on. There was a distance she maintained around her.

I picked up the cash. "You want a receipt?"

"I think all of our transaction should be paperless, don't you?"

"If you can arrange it," I said. "How do you see closing the deal? Cash in a dark alley and delivery of the sword?"

"Cash will work—and it will be in a lawyer's office with security. BitCoins work as well. I will bring the sword. You bring the cash and the buyer. You get your commission on the spot."

"You know this could take some time to find the perfect buyer," I said. "What is our time frame?"

"Immediately," Carolyn said, motioning her arm around the room. "These surroundings are not cheap."

"I'd better get started then," I said.

"Text me your progress," she said, turning to the housekeeper. "Rosa, would you show Mr. Kugar the door."

Chapter 9

On the drive down the Pacific Coast Highway toward Ventura, the impact sunk in of what I had taken on. I was to broker the most famous sword in the world, and I suspected the most valuable. Along the way I had to keep it a secret from two governments.

There have been famous swords all through history, swords attributed to magical powers and strengths. King Authur's Excalibur being one of the first—but it had been returned to the lake from which it came, and nothing but a myth.

The Honjo Masamume was real. It existed and had been passed down through the ruling generations of Japan for 400 years.

Japanese swords are not a specialty of mine, but I do have a working knowledge. My first introduction was at a South Carolina knife and gun show and a gray-haired man walked by with a sword on his shoulder. My tablemate was a wheeler-dealer. "How much on the Samurai?" he asked. The man stopped and approached the table. I could see the tsuba was gold but remained silent.

"Five hundred dollars," he said.

"Where did you get it?"

"Off a dead Jap general on Okinawa," he said. I rolled my eyes. Every Japanese sword coming through a knife show in those days had come from a dead Japanese general on some Pacific island. I always thought it curious that there were a lot of generals on those islands—and wondered aloud why Japanese colonels and captains did not seem to have swords.

My companion peeled off five one hundred-dollar bills and put the sword under the table. Two days later he called me. "I asked Charlie and his wife to come over and look at the sword. Charlie likes them, and I hoped his wife, who is Japanese, could read the tang."

"Yes, what did he say?"

"Charlie took one look at the sword and told me that once a sword gets over $20,000 in value, he is not qualified to appraise it. His wife was so excited that she brought some sword powder back to me to clean it that afternoon."

"20 grand? Did you sell it?"

"Not yet. I'm holding out for more." My companion was an importer and ended up trading the sword for $50,000 in merchandise from his Japanese supplier. The Japanese supplier had sought out the family whose General had carried it off to war and were delighted to have it returned to the family—for the six-figure fee the supplier charged them. That was enough to spur my interest in Japanese swords. I read a few books, had some conversations with exhibitors of swords at a few shows. I knew what I was dealing with. The Honjo Masamume was the holy grail of Japanese swords.

Chapter 10

I value what I call windshield time. Alone in a car without major distractions other than traffic. It gives me time to think with the radio off and a minimum of outside distractions.

As I drove away from Santa Barbara, I answered some of my own questions. Why did she choose me? It was more than Bob's single estate reference I suspected. There are several people who specialize in fine Japanese swords—but there would be too much at risk to use one of them.

In one of the long sweeping curves, I saw brown dots in the ocean to my right. I saw the dark heads of seals in the surf, playing, waiting for fish to come by for their meal. I wondered if this Carolyn, this Carolyn IV, might be like that, playing, and I was the fish.

I turned on the radio to classic oldies. The radio was playing "Hollywood Nights" by Bob Seeger. I ran through my mind the differences between me at this moment and the Midwestern boy in the song, seeing that beautiful face and losing all control. There were not enough differences, but I pushed it out of my mind and went back to the analysis of what the real priority was here.

Any well-known dealer in Japanese swords who could secure and return the Honjo Masamune would have more to gain from finding favor with the Japanese government and the wealthy industrialists in Japan than they would the dollars from a one-time transaction. The ego gratification would be too much to resist, to be forever more known as the dealer who had rediscovered the Honjo Masamune sword. I have long ago learned that the ego can be an expensive proposition.

If the sword's rediscovery became known and was tied to her, Carolyn IV would have to prove clear ownership of the sword – and likely some lawyer or government bureaucrat would seize it to get a little glory of their own, leaving Carolyn, and me, nothing.

And the one overriding question I could not answer as I drove is why with my history, I was having anything to do with a woman named Carolyn.

Chapter 11

I spread the photographs out on the Marriott hotel bed, putting them together to show all five photographs lined up in larger than life-size. Then I took out the copy of the hamon line from the Honjo, that Carolyn had blown up to match the size of the photos.

Taking each photo in turn, I held it up to the light against the archive drawing of the temper line, the hamon—and there it was, a dead match. That could not be duplicated.

Few people care about the hamon line compared to another hamon line, unless the sword is a priceless National Treasure. Then artists copied that hamon line minutely, and thus the fingerprint for the genuine Honjo Masamune exists to verify the sword's authenticity.

Chapter 12

Carolyn III was my expensive Carolyn, both in dollars and in emotional toil. I married her. I have always gone after very attractive women. My theory is you can be with a beautiful woman or an average woman—either way, you still must look at them.

That thought must be tempered with the goal of a pretty woman with the personality of an average looking woman. That is the desired prize. I thought I had found that.

If you consider the pretty women we know and the insecurities they all seem to have about their appearance, imagine the hole most average women must be in, enduring a world of sports magazines with supermodels and a deluge of skinny beautiful women on the nightly news and in movies.

Average looking women recognize that they have to offer more than looks—with sincerity, good nature, and letting their sweetness show through. I say that knowing that everyone has a different opinion of what is beautiful.

A pretty woman with an average woman attitude, that was what I desired. The fact that on some occasions my Carolyn, Carolyn III hushed the room when she made an entrance only added gasoline to my fire.

We met in college, love at first sight and then confirmed when I learned her name. I still had a blind side to the name. Later, after the divorce was finalized, and my near self-destruction as I self-medicated with vast quantities of Kentucky bourbon when my friends would learn I was dating someone, their first question would be, "Is her name Carolyn?"

"No."

"Good, enjoy," they would say. They were keeping the Carolyn caution in my mind for my own safety, I knew.

Carolyn III and I had good years, years of bliss, I thought. We married early in college and began building careers, her in graphic design, me in advertising, and there came a time when the conversation came around to kids, a house, a mortgage. I was all for it. I thought she was too. But there was something holding her back. I couldn't put my finger on it, so I convinced her it was what we should do, become the typical American family, and she relented.

Two kids, a boy, and a girl, and a mortgage, and the realization that the potential I thought I once had maybe I didn't have. With the cutbacks in one of those downturns in the economy and the loss of my real job I settled into buying and selling to pay bills with grandiose plans of importing, exporting, and dabbling with furnishing rare and expensive toys to the wealthy and privileged.

Chapter 13

My cell rang and aware of the stringent talking-on-the-phone-while-driving laws in California, I pulled to the side at the first turn off and returned the call. It was Daniel in Costa Mesa, checking to be sure I was on for dinner. We ate Mexican, and between chips and salsa, I told him what I could. "This is a well-known sword," I said, "but it is important that part of it not be known initially."

"Why is that?" My friend asked.

"Sometimes you ask questions I cannot answer," I said.

"How would you identify one sword from the other, does it have their names on them?"

"On some," I said. "But the hamon line, the temper line, is as identifiable as a fingerprint." I caught the puzzled look and knew I had to explain. His wife Peggy saw what was coming.

"Oh hell, here we go, another book lesson," she said, rolling her eyes. She smiled over at her husband. "Daniel, it appears someone had drunk all my Cosmo while I wasn't looking. I am going to the bar for a refill and leave you two guys to talk about things in which I have absolutely no interest. I'll be back." She rose and disappeared into the ornately carved wood entrance of the bar.

"OK, go on," Daniel said. "First how do you know all this?"

"Because a few years ago I was invited to the Seki City Cutlery Fair near Gifu, Japan. There is a swordmaking demonstration, and I asked a lot of questions through an interpreter. Once the sword master saw my sincere interest, he invited me to his shop for a couple of days."

"OK, so you made swords?"

"No, I took a lot of photos and did a lot of listening. He was not a master for nothing. But I did learn the process," I said.

"Like the hamon line?"

"Yes, like the hamon line. A Japanese sword begins as a clump of metal about the size of a fist, special layers of high and low carbon steel called tamahagane." Daniel nodded.

"Then as the master taps with a small hammer his two assistants with large hammers strike where the master has tapped, hammering and stretching the steel until it is drawn out, folded, drawn out again, and eventually layers with a softer outer shell wrapping the blade except for the edge of the steel.

"Each strike of the hammer moves the molecules of the steel in a unique manner, all which is revealed when in the final stages of the forging process the blade is quenched, wrapped in clay and other ingredients depending on the sword maker. Some use rust, or dust from polishing stones, but always clay and water. The thickness of the clay is based on how hard the master wants that part of the blade to be. The edge is harder and receives a thinner coating, while the thicker upper part of the blade gets more clay, making it that part of the steel softer and more flexible.

"As the blade is tempered and left to cool, the natural effect adds the smooth curve to the blade. A blade quenched quickly in water changes the steel structure to martensite, a hard form of steel, and creating a temper line where the hard steel and softer steel meet, giving sword has a unique hamon (temper) line."

"So the temper line cannot be pre-designed?"

"No, the interaction of the steels as they harden is what makes it unique. The end results look like a side view of the ocean, each wave is a different spacing, a different height, the line a different thickness," I explained.

"Interesting," Daniel said, watching his wife approach and indicating his lack of interest in hearing more.

"I can't say much more than that. Just put the feelers out that you know of a nice Japanese sword. You know any Japanese sword collectors with deep pockets? They would have to be very big collectors?" I asked.

"We have a few come in the store, a couple inspired by those Kill Bill movies and that old Bodyguard movie with Kevin Costner. They would pay a few thousand for something really nice, I suspect that would be it."

"I need a special buyer then. Someone outside the norm. Outside our circles."

"I will keep an ear out, but I don't expect anything to turn up."

"How are you doing otherwise?" Peggy asked.

"Waiting on another Carolyn?" Daniel joked. Peggy shot him daggers. She had liked Carolyn III.

***

I never made a secret of the angst in my life and the horrors inflicted upon my psyche by women named Carolyn. I cried on the shoulders of many friends—usually when it was too many drinks, late at night around a campfire, or stuck on some dusty outpost in the black night waiting for someone to stumble into our ambush.

I recognized my weakness for Carolyns and had no hesitation to give my history of all three. I think it was not easing the pain by talking about it, but more for my own safety, for my friends to remind me in moments of weakness that I had a recurring problem with women named Carolyn. Daniel and Peggy were within my circle of confidants about my Carolyn issues.

"I hope I am through with Carolyns," I said. I didn't add that I had hours earlier entered a business deal with a beautiful woman named Carolyn. They would not understand.

"After the last one you damn well better hope you are," Daniel said. "Live and learn."

"You hear from her anymore?" Peggy asked.

"Not after she landed full custody of the kids and has to give permission for me to see them," I said.

"That's tough, I know," Peggy said.

"Tougher than you'd ever know. I just hope she doesn't poison them on me before they get big enough to make up their own minds."

***

That night in my hotel room I fired up my laptop and emailed all my contacts for references to buyers who could handle a seven or eight figure item.

After that and not sleepy, I began searching for Carolyn McMasters. She was born in Arizona, 37 years old unless she was fudging for her IMBD profile, bit parts in a half-dozen unmemorable TV shows five years ago, a secretary who brought coffee to the boss in one show, a dispatcher who brought the BOLO to the detective in another, 20 seconds of her image on the screen.

So brief that no one would really notice unless it was an old friend from the hometown or a parent or grandparent who would record it and show it every time company came, turning on the TV, calling up the show, and bracing everyone as those 20 seconds appeared. "Here it comes, watch for it, Shussh," and then the satisfied "Ahhh" when the moment was over, always followed with, "I don't know why they won't give her a better part."

There are servers and bartenders all over LA with that identical resume.

Under the "Images" search most of the photos were from years earlier, judging from the hairstyles, and she was maybe eight or nine pounds thinner, with a variety of hair colors ranging from a maroon red to a dark brunette, although most were in the light brown she currently wore.

Carolyn McMasters had two speaking roles in two B-grade movies, one in which she played a hooker who gets caught in bed with the husband of a jealous wife and is killed on the spot, the other role was the girlfriend of one of the outlaws who gets arrested in the first 10 minutes.

In the hooker role, there was a link to celebrity skin site that shows her stripping off her top in a grainy blurred sequence.

I had watched neither movie but did a quick search of the movies and read the summaries. She had no credits in the past three years.

Carolyn's one marriage ended when her husband Joseph DeLacroix overdosed on heroin in the company of two 19-year-olds at a rundown Venice Beach bungalow, and he didn't recover. It seems one of the girls was cheating on her husband and walked out on the dying Joseph rather than call for help. That was two years ago.

Her Facebook page and Twitter accounts said little. Facebook was private, you had to be approved by her for access, and on Twitter, she only made a few comments on movies and congratulations or two for someone's movie award. She followed most of the studios, a few photographers, and a hand full of actors and actresses I recognized.

Prior addresses were Arizona, Austin, TX, Los Angeles, UC Santa Barbara then LA again for a few years, and now back in Santa Barbara.

From the dates, I assumed the move to Santa Barbara was when she and her late husband had bought the house. I delved into his background.

DeLacroix had more movie roles than his wife and was 10 years older. He directed a couple of movies, some fame and some big returns for a short while. But his star faded. From the gossip columns, he spent a lot of the money he earned in his heyday as powder crammed up his nose. I stopped searching. The pair of them was too much of what I call Typical California egocentric celebrity disorder—no one happy or satisfied with anything they had, and arrogance toward anyone who was not in the same world, something I had witnessed firsthand earlier that morning.

Chapter 14

My wife, Carolyn III, did not have California egocentric celebrity disorder, but she became completely on board with being unhappy and dissatisfied with everything in our marriage. Child rearing turned out tougher than she expected. She had never had a strong constitution, so she was constantly fatigued, despite a gym-rat workout schedule that kept her tight body fit. Still, she searched. She took hands full of vitamins, health foods, yoga, looking for something that would bring more satisfaction to the state of her life. And then one night her search focused in a more private direction, what I call "the conversation."

We had been invited to a party with some of her friends from the gym. "I do not want you walking into anything blind," she said. "Some of them are swingers."

"As in wife-swappers?"

"Yes."

"And are we expected to participate?" I asked.

"No, no, nothing like that. Only don't be surprised by what you see there. They are friends because they are friends, not because of what they do with their own personal lives."

"How many of the friends you work out with are into this?"

"Four."

"Out of a group of how many?" I asked.

"Five who have coffee every morning."

"Five plus you?"

"No, five including me." Her innocent look had long since stopped being effective on me. I knew there was an agenda but despite what I already knew, I had no idea what her agenda was.

"So, every morning you sit and have coffee with these four women, all talking about their sexual liaisons with each other's spouses?"

"Not exactly," Carolyn III said.

"Huh?"

"Well some of them are not restricted to other people's spouses, they enjoy other outside partners as well. It is called hotwifing."

"While their husbands do what exactly?"

"Watch. Wait at home for the descriptions of what happened. Or if it is a swap, they are playing with someone themselves." I watched her face as she told me this. Too much animation in her movements and face. She was intrigued.

"We married young. You didn't have the opportunity to enjoy a lot of different partners," I said.

"I know."

"Do your friends know?"

"Yes."

"You told them?" I asked.

"Yes. They all feel sorry for me."

"And they are encouraging you and I to get into their little group of swingers?"

"If we want to, we would be welcome," Carolyn said. "A couple of my friends have commented that they think you are cute." I was speechless. I needed a drink and got one quickly at the dinner, a tall one, three fingers of Kentucky bourbon.

"And where are you on all this?" Carolyn looked down at the table for a minute then up with a hopeful expression.

"I think it might be fun to try once. If you didn't object." There it was. Not asking my permission but saying she wanted to if I did not object, leaving it to me to be the naysayer.

"That's why you've been so down lately?"

"It has nothing to do with you, Max," she said. "I just wonder. I've always wondered. Talking to the girls has made me wonder more. We are in a rut, it might help, bring some excitement back."

"What do you want to do?"

"I want you to let me try it. I want you to try it. Just once. If we don't like it, we'll stop, I promise. At least go with an open mind and meet some of the people involved."

As I mentioned somewhere in this narrative, I'm a sucker for a woman named Carolyn—especially one I am in love with. What could it hurt just once? Against my gut, I agreed. "OK, we can go to the party at least."

My excited thankful wife showered me with kisses and drug me off to the bedroom for an early evening romp. I remember thinking that if this was the result what she was wanting to try might not be a totally bad thing. I was wrong.

***

My wife and I attended the party, and we met a lot of nice people, much like us, with kids, mortgages, average jobs, and a yearning to add some excitement to their rut lives and searching for that excitement and stimulation in sexual ways.

Freida, one of her gym buddies, was of Germanic origin and looked it. Tall, blonde, and a little top heavy in a good way. She took a liking to me, laughed at my wisecracks at the right time, and was an accountant. "Not your stereotypical accountant," she said. With Carolyn's encouragement and as couples were pairing up for the evening, my wife did some matchmaking, and I was sent off for the night with my least-reluctant choice, Frieda.

I cannot lie, someone new and different, a totally different body style and shape, different reactions to touches, different perfume and tastes, different moans, grunts and whimpers, and the energetic excitement of someone new and the cuddling afterglow with our bodies spent combined with the relaxing effect of a night of drinking—it was great during the act. It was a blur of twisted limbs and the urgent passion seeking release.

Then came the morning as I sobered up and lay in bed with this strange woman wondering what in the hell had I done. I felt guilty, but you cannot unfuck someone. I was also crazy wondering where Carolyn might be and in whose bed she spent the night.

I had been assured by the half-dozen people I talked to before I left with Frida that Carolyn would be fine, they would be sure she was safe and got home OK. She looked me square in the face before I walked out the door and told me the same thing, with a "Have a good time, see you tomorrow."

Frieda was as hung over as I was, bringing much-needed Sprite from the kitchen and painkillers she scrounged from her purse. She was very nice, attractive, friendly, but not Carolyn. "Eat the banana too," she said. "If you don't, the pain killers will tear up your stomach. They're prescription."

I did as instructed. She smiled at me. "Look, I enjoyed last night, and would love to do it again sometime, but the way I'm feeling this morning I don't think a morning fuck is in the cards, do you?" I shook my head no.

"Good. Why don't we get dressed and I run you home? My kids will be coming back from a sleepover at 10."

Frieda grinned, "This is your first time, so I bet you and Carolyn are going to have some fun catching up to do. The first fuck with your spouse after you spend the night with someone else is some of the best sex the two of you will ever have."

Frieda stood in front of me in nude no-tan-lined magnificence, making no effort to cover herself, but with a body such as hers, there was no reason she should be covered. I remember thinking, "Wow, I've just spent the night in the bed enjoying that body."

Frieda dropped me off at home. My SUV was not in the driveway. I went into the empty house. The kids were at Carolyn's parents for the weekend, and I went upstairs for a hot shower. By the time I finished my hangover was easing, and I heard the familiar sound of my SUV pulling up in the driveway.

I went to the upstairs window and looked down into the vehicle that had pulled in behind Carolyn. It was a big dark black Cadillac Escalade, driven by a man as big and black as the vehicle he was driving. He had rolled down his window and Carolyn walked back to him, opening his door and stepping into the space of the half-opened door. She kissed him, her left-hand snaking into his lap as he put a hefty arm around her shoulder and pulled her closer, his right hand moving to fondle her chest.

They broke the embrace and she stepped away. He closed the door and she waited until he had backed into the street and she watched as he drove away before picking up the paper, checking the mailbox and stepping inside.

"Hey, you're already home. Sorry, I'm a little late," my wife gushed. "Did you have a good time with Frieda? Everyone says she's great."

"I did," I said. "You?"

"Oh my God. Unbelievable. I had no idea. You know who I was with? Dante Longfellow. She giggled, "And he was aptly named." It wasn't until she giggled that I realized she was still buzzed.

"You still drinking?" I asked.

"Never stopped. All night. We started on mimosas this morning. I hope he doesn't get stopped by the cops. That's why he followed me home. He played for the Cowboys three years and the Redskins two. He was a defensive end." She looked up at my face. "Yes, he was black. I had always wondered—now I know. Thank you for that."

"You know I don't care if he was black, green, or orange as far as that goes," I said. "It just felt weird for me this morning. I was worried when you were not here."

"I'm here now baby," my wife said, moving closer, alcohol heavy on her breath. "Take me upstairs and reclaim me. All the girls say this is the best part."

That was what I did. And she was right, it was good in a gritty stale sweaty way as if I was determined to erase the memory of someone else who had enjoyed the most private reservations of my marriage and of my wife.

As we clung to each other's sweating bodies, she proceeded to give me a graphic and detailed description of the previous night for her—and this morning too. From her description, she had not had much sleep.

Carolyn III said she had little interest in hearing of my time with Frieda and begged for time to take a nap. I was sweaty from our lovemaking, and showered downstairs for a second time that day.

We did not talk more about it until the following Wednesday when Carolyn III announced there was another party this weekend. "I thought you said it was a one-time thing?" I asked.

"I asked if we could at least try it one time. I would like to do it some more, just for a little while. You enjoyed it too, didn't you baby?"

"I think it is dangerous," I said.

"You are always thinking things are too dangerous," she said. "You are such an old spoilsport," she pouted.

"I don't think we should go," I said.

"That's not a 'no'" Carolyn III smiled. She stopped smiling when I said it a different way.

"OK. How about hell no. No fucking way. I don't want other men fucking my wife. Is that clear enough for you?" I said.

I was too loud I know, from the way she teared up and ran out of the room. Something inside my brain said I should go apologize, but something else in my psyche said I had done nothing for which I should apologize.

We did not attend the party.

Chapter 15

I was home from California and back in my Carolina mountains two days later, heavy on the phone working all my contacts and coming up dry for serious sword buyers. I started calling friends of friends, calling in markers for the names, numbers, and introductions of anyone and everyone who had very deep pockets, a fetish about owning things no one else owned, and that little bit of delight in the illegal. I was discovering a larger market than I had anticipated—but the trick was connecting with the right someone who fit that criteria and someone I could trust. That pool was much smaller.

I contacted everyone I knew in my extended family that had ever worked in Japan, including a cousin who was working there now doing something he couldn't talk about out of the American embassy.

My chocolate lab, Street, wasn't used to seeing me work quite so hard and looked up from time to time and stared rather than curling up and sleeping in front of my desk as usual. He sensed there was no need to bring his throw toy for us to play with outside.

There was a text on my phone that morning. I do not get a lot of texts. It was from Carolyn McMasters. "Told brother. Urgent. We need to talk. Can you come back?"

"I was just out there, no. I do not want to make two flights to California within a week." I texted in return. "Phone?" Her answer was instant.

"No calls. Pick me up at the Atlanta airport tomorrow. I'll text the flight and time."

That quick response and willingness to come to me set me back a second. In for a penny, in for a pound, I texted back. "OK, see you then."

Chapter 16

I waited at the Hartsfield/Jackson airport in the roped off area between the limo drivers holding signs with the names of their arriving fares and the restrooms. I watched one group with a banner welcoming a returning soldier in a clean uniform except for the still dusty boots. Others walked by concentrated on only finding their baggage claim carousel, and far too many were rushing by in a brisk step when, if they had thought about it for a second, had no reason to be rushing.

Carolyn had texted when her plane touched down, and I responded that I was there and waiting. I focused on the emerging line of humanity being shoved into the lobby by the escalator, like sausage pouring out of a grinder.

I was expecting a Hollywood entrance from Carolyn, dressed a little too fancy, too hot, a headscarf and dark sunglasses. You know, Gloria Swanson old school glamorous.

I was not expecting to see a cute woman in a ball cap, matching blue sweatshirt and pants, athletic shoes, and dark-rimmed glasses. She still was gorgeous; there was no way to hide that. As she neared, I saw she was not wearing make-up. She looked wholesome.

Carolyn seemed more relaxed than she had been in her home, despite the six-hour flight and a three-hour time difference. She even half-smiled as she saw my face, not a glad-to-see-you smile but one that hinted at relief. Her entire demeanor was a 100% reversal of the aloof arrogance I had witnessed in California.

"What's the matter, Max? Not what you were expecting?"

"Uh well no, I mean," I stammered before finally getting out, "Have a good flight?"

"No. It was shit actually. I had to take my contacts out because my eyes dry out on planes, I didn't remember until I got on the plane. I went through hell at the security because I paid cash for the ticket. They don't like that. Do I look like a terrorist to you?"

"If you are, you are the best-looking terrorist I've ever seen," I said. Carolyn stopped and smiled a weak smile. "Finally. A compliment. You do have it in you, don't you?" I smiled inward. So, the lady was not used to a lack of attention from men and it bothered her if a man did not follow as she expected—and I was no exception.

"I try to control myself when I'm talking business with a prospective client."

"I wasn't fishing for a compliment." Liar, I thought.

"I didn't think you were. You do seem more relaxed than you were in California."

"Relieved is a better word." She said nothing more, I could see fear returning to her face. "Let's get out of here, please."

"Yes Ma'am"

"I knew that "Ma'am" was coming sooner or later. You Southern boys," she said.

"Guilty as charged. Have you eaten? Drop you off at a hotel?

"Neither. What do you recommend?"

"How are you for burgers?"

"I love a good hamburger," she said. "In-N-Out?"

"Huh?"

"In-N-Out, they make some of the best burgers in LA. They're a chain."

"Actually, I was thinking of something else," I said. "You trust me?"

"Looks like I have to," she said. "Lead on."

After picking up her two heavy bags at the baggage claim, she donned sunglasses in the car as we drove to one of my favorite restaurants near the airport, hanging on by their fingernails after the closing of the old Ford assembly plant. It was, Armandos, known for burgers of fresh ground beef in thick 1/3-pound patties and onion rings that are fresh out of the peanut oil when served. Carolyn removed her sunglasses and replaced them with her oversize black plastic rim eyeglasses. She looked bookish, like a sexy librarian. I liked the look but didn't say so.

We took seats behind the room divider, hidden from the line of customers at the door.

She devoured her burger. "Damn, this is good," she said. "Hard to get this much hot grease on anything in LA. Hell half the things they call burgers have big portobello mushrooms on them instead. Thanks for recommending this. You're doing good so far, Mr. Kugar."

"Max," I said.

"OK, Max," she smiled. "But I bet you keep calling me "Ma'am" from time to time too. You can't help it."

"Probably," I said. "You said we had to meet face to face. Sounds ominous."

Carolyn's face went ashen and she glanced around, her head moving in quick jerks. "Not here." I saw her shoulder shudder a little. "It is ominous." She looked into my eyes. "I didn't want any trace of being here. That was why I paid cash and asked you to pick me up. I have nowhere else to go with my problem—and it involves you too."

A customer paused beside our table waiting for his wife to catch up and Carolyn stopped talking. "I will explain later," she said glancing up at the man.

"Where do you plan to go from here?"

"I have no idea." This was the first time I noticed a crack in her hard shell. I saw vulnerability there.

"Do you have a hotel room in Atlanta?" She shook her head no.

"I'm trying to not leave a credit card trail. You have any ideas?"

"Couple of options," I said. "I can rent you a room in a hotel here in Atlanta using my credit card, or I have a few places at home, up in the mountains that I look after for out-of-state owners. They wouldn't mind a house sitter for a day or two."

"Ideal," she said. "We'll talk in the car."

Chapter 17

Carolyn didn't speak until we turned off the I-75 from the northbound lane to the feeder road toward the mountains. "You told me in California that you hunted. Is that true?"

"Yes."

"You have guns?" I laughed.

"Is that funny?"

"You are asking a Southerner raised in the Carolina mountains that question? Yes, I have guns. I have a lot of guns."

Carolyn settled back in the seat with a satisfied expression, looking out the window. "Good," she said. "I hope you will not need them." I waited for her to continue, my mind screaming what the fuck, but I still played it cool for the moment. She changed the subject as we passed the Woodstock exit.

"You used to live near here, right?" she said as we passed the Woodstock exit.

"Yes."

"I remembered it because it has the same name as that famous music festival."

"Yes."

"Why do you not live here now?" Carolyn asked.

"Wife got the house and I went home, like John Muir said, 'The mountains are calling, and I must go.' Huntington is a small lazy town in the Carolina mountains. I was born and raised there."

"Messy divorce?"

"Nothing I care to talk about," I said.

"Why did you go back to the mountains," she asked. "Running back home?"

"You left out 'with my tail tucked between my legs' but yeah, it was something like that. I needed a refuge, a place to regroup, so I went home. Mom and Dad were gone, I had a small place there and a little commercial building that would house my business—and," I paused as the sadness of that time swept over me in a wave, "I had nowhere else to go."

Chapter 18

Returning home to recover from a divorce was the least likely place to go, and had I any other place to run to, I would have gone there.

Most of my friends from my Huntington youth escaped at the same time I did, shortly after high school, and never went back. We called it escaping when we would get together at the class reunions every five years.

The few that remained were deep into the small-town life and would shrink back when the conversations of their classmates turned to escaping the dull drab little town.

What became apparent in my first week back home was the place I had escaped was not the place to which I had returned—at least at first glance.

Over the years thanks to crime, hurricanes, and a boom in land prices, Oconaluftee County had experienced an invasion of Floridians looking for mountain vistas, a quieter life, or in some instances cashing in on the family homestead after the parents died and flee to the mountains. What they didn't realize was the Floridians they thought they were escaping were on their heels chasing them to the mountains for their own piece of land in the sky.

After five or six years in Huntington, the former outlanders typically began demanding many of the same things for which they had left Florida in the first place, trying to force their will over that of natives who had lived in the area for generations. creating new friction and two different camps and ways of thought.

The real estate agents tried to walk the razor's edge, and many, like myself, preferred to stay neutral.

So what if the Floridians tired of carrying their garbage to dumpsters rather than a curbside pickup, and those Florida desires—and whining-- was a constant refrain at the county commissioners' meeting.

This massive influx was welcomed with open arms by the local real estate agents, the economy boomed for real estate and construction. The need to follow the money meant the real estate schools were crammed, to the point that it became a local joke that to return home required one to obtain a real estate license.

Before the 2008 crash, a few fortunes were made— and after the crash, those same fortunes vanished as fast as the morning mountain mists in the sunshine.

My first day back home at the lone health club in town, I struck up conversations with a dozen people, not a one a native, all from Florida before coming here, including some from New York, to Florida and then to Carolina, referred to non-affectionately as "half-backs". Some had insulated themselves into the local bureaucracy and began to effect changes that broke my once backward hometown out of its old traditional mold.

That same afternoon the waitress at the coffee shop with a sharp Northern accent called me a "salmon." "A lot of you are coming back," she said, "just like a salmon going upstream to where they were born."

"Hopefully not to die," I joked, but my joke faded as I realized that should I live a normal life and die of natural causes, whether heart attack, stroke, or car accident, I would indeed likely die here.

I recalled what a comedian once said about the likely chance if you were going to be involved in a serious auto accident it would be within 25 miles of home and I repeated it to the waitress to explain my return. "So, I moved!" he said.

The waitress didn't laugh, oblivious to my trying to be friendly. She didn't say thank you when she returned with my change either. She uttered "boomerang" under her breath but loud enough to hear as she turned away.

***

"I've never spent much time in the mountains," Carolyn McMasters said as we weaved through the mountain curves. "I was born in the desert and usually lived on the coast."

"Brace yourself for some culture shock," I grinned.

Chapter 19

There was too much pain involved in telling Carolyn McMasters why I was divorced. They say time heals, but the end of my marriage is still a raw open wound with me, and time has not helped.

It was four months after the swinging party in Woodstock and my night with Frieda. I discovered Carolyn III's extra phone. It was not on my Verizon plan, and I was fearful of what it meant.

I came home early on a Wednesday thanks to a back strain from helping a co-worker move a desk, with the Doc's recommendation of soaking in a hot bath to relieve the back spasms. I heard a phone chirp with an unusual chime from Carolyn's chair.

We both had Samsungs, and this was an Apple. At first, I thought someone had left it at the house, some friend stopping by and it falls out of a purse. That was until the text came in as I held it.

"Hey baby just wanted to tell you that you are my vanilla shorty. The best. Can't wait until Friday and I can hit it all night long."

I scrolled up to read an earlier message sent to the sender by my wife. "I can still feel the sensation of you inside me even though it has been four hours since I left my chocolate bar. I'm addicted," it read. I noted the number, and after an hour online, I knew a name, address, where he worked, and the name of his ex-wife. He was the ex-football player from that first night, Dante Longfellow.

I am a simple buyer and seller of specialty items, but a life of interacting with forgers, liars, criminals, and the dishonest soon teaches one to be cautious and to realize there is no such thing as a coincidence. I do not believe in coincidence.

I knew what that phone meant but I was in denial. Not my wife, not my Carolyn. My denial failed to prevent a part of me, a massive chunk of my romantic heart, from dying.

My mind was blank, and my body numb, I slid the phone back beside the seat cushion.

Carolyn III heard me downstairs and came bouncing down the steps with a perky smile, rushing to me and giving me a hug. "You're home early." She smelled fresh and a hint of soap as if she had just had a shower.

"Strained my back," I said. "Doc said to soak in a hot bath."

"Oh baby, I'm sorry. You go up and run you a bath and I'll bring you a drink. I have to run out for a minute to pick up something for supper, all right?"

"OK." She brought back my drink, a tall one, and set it down beside the tub. I had not stepped into the tub yet.

"This should help," she said. "I might be a while." I heard the door slam and her car pull away. I gave her a 30 count and eased down the stairs to her chair, sliding my hand beside the cushion. The Apple phone was gone.

***

My plans had been to attend a trade show in Cincinnati, staying over for Friday and Saturday night. The trip was a dreary and boring eight-hour drive from Woodstock, necessitating an early morning departure on Friday.

I called Thursday morning and canceled my room at Home2. I didn't cancel the tables. They were paid for and would reflect that if anyone checked to see if I was there. Thursday night Carolyn came over and eased down beside me on the couch. "How's your back?" she asked.

"Better, but still sore," I said.

"Why don't you stretch out here and let me rub it for you with some Icy Hot."

"That would be nice." I stretched out and yielded to her kneading hands and the warming cream.

"That feels better baby," I answered with a soft moan of pleasure.

"Good," she said, continuing. "You still going to Ohio tomorrow? You are feeling OK for that?"

"Yeah, I have to go," I said. "Couple of important clients are to meet me there."

"OK, well I have to go to the gym early for a class, so if I miss you when you leave have a good trip. You coming back Sunday?" she asked.

"Yeah, as usual," I deadpanned.

"Now you go to bed right now with your back relaxed," she said.

"I will. I'm beat," I said. Carolyn III remained downstairs. Our house was old, with creaking floors, but when you have lived in a house as long as I had in that one, it was not a problem to step in the spots that it would not creak.

I crept to the banister and looked over to the living room below. I had to lean over to see Carolyn, and she was rapidly texting on the Apple phone—no doubt confirming her hook-up.

I felt like crying but instead, I was in such a fury that as I lay in bed I plotted and fumed mayhem and destruction until the fatigue and stress wore me down and I finally drifted to sleep, dreaming of the pain and misery I wanted to inflict rather than suffering that pain and misery myself. Such plotting moments are when I am my most dangerous, my thoughts devoid of compassion and filled only with bitter cruel rage. I have usually managed to control those black feelings. This was not one of those times.

***

That morning I loaded the packed bag I take to shows, filled my Yeti cup to the brim with strong hot coffee and drove away from Woodstock, going North, but not toward Cincinnati. Instead it was 515 all the way to my friend Vernon's 24-foot camper parked three hours away, back at my childhood home on the lake in Huntington, North Carolina.

Vernon loaned me his camper for the weekend. He is addicted to fishing and makes that camper his home during the summer. He had a dock for his bass boat a few feet away from the camper door so he could be fishing first thing by stepping a few feet from the camper and on to his tricked-out boat.

His wife Irene tried to understand his compassion but after a while trying to fish with him and camp, she gave up on enjoying fishing herself and began to tolerate rather than participate in his obsession. She would visit on weekends, remaining at their home during the week since she still had her day job.

Vernon was not using the camper this time of year, as the TVA had drawn down the lake to reveal bare brown clay banks. His dock rested on the ground and his bass boat was under a cover in his garage, waiting for the lake to rise in the spring.

I told him I would be alone, but I had lied. I had brought two old friends with me: Jack Daniels and Jim Beam.

I swapped cars with Vernon, borrowing his keys to the old black Chevy truck he leaves at the campsite. He calls the truck "Blackie" and refers to it only as "my hunting and fishing truck." The black finish bears the scratches of the narrow mountain trails from brush scraping both sides. Vernon prefers going into the rough high country for native trout.

At 11 p.m. Friday night, in Blackie, I drove back to Woodstock. I passed by my house, and parked two doors down. Everything looked normal, no one was outside, and the glow from the televisions flashed black and white against the open curtained living rooms.

Wearing a black hoodie, I eased across my neighbor's fresh cut yard, the neighbor who prefers cats and does not have a dog. I pressed my hand against the glass of the closed overhead garage door and peered into my garage.

This was the deciding moment, that instant that could confirm my fears or make me feel like an idiot for doubting my wife. It could go many ways and I still bore a glimmer of hope.

My side of the garage could be empty, all my discoveries up to this point could be explained as my making a mistake. An old girlfriend's car could be inside, someone who would always bitch at Carolyn about how she was not living up to her potential by settling for me— she had a couple of those friends and never made it a known thing when she met them. I preferred not to know.

She could have invited them for a sleepover and bitch-about-Max session.

Or inside my garage could be a car I didn't recognize, again something that might have a logical explanation. The worst would be all my suspicions were true and a black Escalade would be parked inside. I peered inside my palm against the window.

I saw the Cadillac emblem first, recognized the Escalade outline, and a part of me died. My knees gave way and I sunk to the ground, struggling to gain control my myself from the stunning shock of betrayal. What I did next was a spur of the moment.

This was my home and my driveway. Her lover was likely sleeping in the bed I paid for, eating my food, drinking my liquor, fucking *my* wife.

So if I chose to fill the expansion joint in the concrete between the garage floor and the outside concrete with upright roofing nails a few inches apart that I retrieved from Blackie's toolbox, that was my own option. It was my property. So, I did. I did not suspect her friend would expect four flats on his Escalade. It would require a tow, and I hoped he did not have Triple-A.

Four flats would be little more than an inconvenience, but setting it up made me feel better for the moment. Anything more in my current mental state would likely land me in jail, and that would solve nothing. I needed to give myself time to be sure I didn't follow my first instinct—homicide.

I sat for long minutes in Vernon's truck, absorbing my shock, before returning to his camper, where I began to renew my acquaintance with friends Mr. Beam and Mr. Daniels.

It was a rough hangover the next morning. I had survived worse nights of drinking, but never a worse night.

Thanks to my loving wife who had stood in front of a church of friends and family years earlier and pledged her life to me, now with her total betrayal I endured the worst night of my life.

All the drinking did was add a headache to the inevitable reality of what I faced the next morning.

Chapter 20

"You are quiet," Carolyn McMasters said as the light faded into shiny black darkness, enveloping us as we rode North through the rainy Georgia night. It must have been a night like this that inspired Tony Joe White's "Rainy Night in Georgia".

The glare from the soaked highway and the incessant passing of car after car with their bright LED headlights was giving me a headache. I had turned down the dash lights as far as I could to reduce the glare, but it helped little.

"Just thinking and wondering," I said. "Why are you here Carolyn? When are you going to get to the reason you are here?"

"It's my half-brother." She said. "We've never been close, but he's still my brother, you know. I wasn't trying to screw him. We were catching up on our monthly call and Thomas was describing this super big deal he has cooking, and how it is going to take a lot of money and he's borrowing against everything he owns for this deal."

"That's nice," I said.

"No, it is not nice. I tried to be nice. I told him about Grandad's sword, and how I was going to sell it and he wouldn't have to worry about the money. I thought he would thank me, but he went crazy. Thomas got into cocaine and other stuff before and went paranoid, and I think he is into it again. He is beyond paranoid. He went berserk."

"He scare you?"

"Damn right he scared me. He was all over the map, completely irrational. First, he demanded the sword; he wants to give it to the Japanese. He's trying to work a deal with a Japanese company and said it would curry favor. Then he wanted to buy it from me, and then while still on the phone he changed his mind again. He said he wanted to destroy the sword so it wouldn't taint his deal."

"And you told him?"

"What do you think I told him?" Carolyn said, her voice rising in timbre.

"Let me guess. You told him to go fuck himself?"

"Precisely. It pissed him off, even more, big time. That's when he promised that he would have that sword or else. He said this deal was the most important thing in his life and he would let nothing stand in the way, even his sister. He said he was coming to LA to get it, and if he didn't get it, he was going to kill me and anyone else I had told about the sword, just to be sure it didn't interfere with his deal. If I did not believe him, just wait and see."

"He's bat shit crazy," I said.

"Yes, he is. But he meant every word. If he wants the sword to go away, he will want everyone who knows anything about the sword to go away too."

"That's insane."

"Yes, it is. That doesn't stop it from being true. Thomas works with the Mexican Cartels; he lets them use some of the family land he inherited down on the border, some with warehouses, and the cartels use them for tunnels or something. He doesn't know I know about that, but he knows some very bad people.

"Thomas scares me; the people he does business with, they scare me—a lot. I know. He has bragged to me that to gain his way into their trust they had videoed him shooting a snitch—in the head. He bragged about it. Thomas has no conscience or love for anything.

"After we hung up, I panicked and decided I had to run. It is my only hope. I called two close girlfriends from my gym. We rushed through my house and loaded all our vehicles as fast as we could with my stuff. I took everything important that I could move easily and stored it my friend Julie's basement.

"My house is still full of furniture and a lot of personal things, but no legal papers or things I value. I couldn't take everything,"

Carolyn continued, "On the way back from her house, my warning light for gas came on in my car and I realized I needed a fill-up. Instead of pulling into my drive, I went to the bottom of the hill first to fill up. As I passed my driveway, I saw a gas company truck and two men standing at my door. I was almost to the gas station before it hit me."

"So?"

"I don't have gas in my house. It's all electric. I called the cops and I didn't go back. I stayed with a friend in LA last night, ran by the bank and got as much cash as I could, borrowing against my credit cards, and caught the plane to here this morning."

"Does your brother know that I know?" I asked.

"Not by name. I told him I had signed with a broker to sell the sword, but he will get my phone records and see I've talked to you. It may take a day or two. He will figure it out. Between him and the cartel people, they can get access to credit card and phone records. I know that because he told me once he could help me find any of my old friends if I needed."

Carolyn looked up at me, her eyes wide. "I had nowhere else to go without involving friends who have nothing to do with this. As you are the only person who knows, and you are in the same danger I am, we're in this together, like it or not."

I was incredulous. "You mean your brother wants to send cartel assassins to kill me simply because I know about a fucking sword I've never seen?"

"I told you he was crazy," Carolyn said.

"Fuck. Where is the sword?"

"A safe place. A place no one would ever look."

"Not even your brother?"

"Especially not my brother. Don't ask. The less you know about that the better."

"Yeah, sometimes it is tough to know too much," I said, remembering the end of my marriage.

Chapter 21

Carolyn III still thought I was in Ohio on Saturday. In Vernon's camper, I waited until Saturday night before returning to my home. Repeating my approach as I had done the previous night, I peered through the garage window again. The Escalade was still there. I looked down at the spacer—all the roofing nails were still intact where I left them. He had not left my home since yesterday.

I heard a giggle from the back yard, inside the fence, near the hot tub. I eased toward the fence, my body against the house and peered through a gap in the fence. There was no need for my caution. My wife and her lover were far too busy engaging in an act to notice my shadow on the fence.

Something else now died further inside me: my sense of well-being, the trust I thought was in our marriage, the comfort of the American dream in which I had wrapped myself. Now in the explicit terms of their two nude intertwined bodies, there was no denial, no fooling myself, no bargaining with the fates that I was not seeing what I was seeing. My heart was decomposing in stages, turning into a black burned up charred piece of meat with little if any heart left.

I considered my options in those seconds, and some of those considerations were as black as my heart. I could let myself in the front door, go to the bedroom, take out my .40 Glock from the safety safe on the nightstand, creep out the back door, and shoot them both in the hot tub. It would only take a couple of rounds each. Tap Tap. Quick. Less blood to clean up that way. Or, I could simply shoot him and then myself. On the other hand, I could quietly steal away and bide my time.

The old saying from a Bernard Cornwall "Sharp" series book stuck in my brain. "Revenge is a dish best eaten cold."

I carefully returned the way I had come and drove back into the welcoming folds of the hollows of my raising. I was too distraught to drink any more Saturday night, but that was when I began to plot my retribution.

\#   \#

Chapter 22

Carolyn McMasters needed to be out of sight, and I had just the place in mind to stash her for the night—a place where no one would find her. I took the narrow gravel mountain road up to the Patterson chalet, going inside first, checking it out, turning on the heat, showing Carolyn McMasters where everything turned on and off. From the chalet, one could see a good mile down the valley for any approaching truck, and there was only a half dozen porch lights visible in the sparse hollow.

To the left, the glow of downtown Huntington lit a half circle of light behind Burger Mountain. Save for the crickets' cacophony outside, the chalet was silent.

The Pattersons had returned to Florida only the week before, so the chalet was fully stocked, right down to the liquor and wine. Even the internet and satellite TV were still connected.

Part of my deal with the owners was I would check on their place periodically, fix anything that might be damaged after a storm or some unforeseen calamity and they would call before they left Florida. That gave me time to get to the chalet, turn on the outside lights, and the air or heat depending on the time of year.

When they went south for the winter, whatever foodstuffs that remained from the summer were mine. They didn't waste and did not like hauling food back and forth. I had not had a chance to clean out their larder, which worked to our advantage now. Then I had kicked myself for something I had not checked.

"Where's your cell phone?" I asked. I didn't need her brother tracking her with it.

"In a trash bin of a bus somewhere in the Southwest."

"What?"

"On the way to the LAX I stopped by the bus station in the valley, spied a man counting out pennies for a bus ticket, and I gave him the phone. I told him it was a burner and only had an hour left on it, to toss it when he was through. He was grateful."

"How did you text me?"

"Burner. Walmart in Oxnard." Carolyn held up a small phone. "You have the number on your phone."

"Burner might be a good idea," I said.

"Max, other than hiding out, which I can't do forever, what am I going to do?" There was a tremble in her voice, a crack in her façade.

"Two options, the way I see it," I said. "We sell the sword and get that off the table or we have a long private one on two with your brother, explain to him the way of the world."

"Or give him the sword?"

"You said giving him the sword will not be enough," I said. "Why is he so adamant about this Japanese deal that he would be willing to kill his own sister."

"As I said, we were never close," Carolyn said as if that explained everything. I continued to stare waiting for the rest.

"Thomas is in the battery industry when he is not sniffing cocaine," she said. "Fancy batteries, the kind that fit in tiny watches and Stinger missiles. He has been working with a Japanese firm, a car firm, a spin-off of Toyota."

"OK."

"They've done it."

"Done what?"

"Created the first truly electric car that is feasible. It recharges from solar panels built into the roof of the car. With the new battery technology of my brother's company, the car works."

"What do you mean, 'works'?"

"Works as in they have run 12 test models in this secret location, and they have been running non-stop for three months. 24 hours a day, stopping only to change drivers. The batteries are that good and charge that easy. It would end fossil fuel cars in 10 years or less."

"And your brother?"

"My brother has secured the exclusive license to import this car to America, once he comes up with enough money. He will have the rights to sell the dealerships, to import the cars, and own the US rights to the patents. This will be bigger than the lightbulb."

"Then why is he concerned…"

"There is one clause, he called it a 'face' clause. His contract is contingent on not doing anything to embarrass the company."

"Like discovering his sister has a Japanese National Treasure sword in her possession."

"Yes."

"Why would a Mexican cartel care if one of their tunnel owners is in a car deal?"

"The Mexican cartel staked him and now own half of my brother's company. They own half the franchise to bring in the cars. My brother is the front man. His problem is they have given him all the money they intend to close the deal, and it's not closed yet. He is on thin ice."

"Oh shit," I said.

"Oh shit is right." She leaned back and closed her eyes as she spoke. I could tell she was crashing.

"No one knows you're here. Try to get a good night's sleep. I'll be here early in the morning," I said.

Chapter 23

In looking back at my marriage to Carolyn III, there are times that I think I would have been better served had I retrieved my pistol and killed my wife and her lover that night. That is all in retrospect. Murdering them would have had complications—and as I pondered that option from the camper, I realized that neither she nor he was not worth those complications.

Instead, I called to our home in Woodstock, Georgia from a motel Sunday night and told Carolyn I had suffered car trouble and they were trying to get me on the road but I might be home tomorrow, but it was possible I might not be home until the day after tomorrow. She aided my plan when she came back with that she had been thinking about a quick run to her sisters for overnight and hated she would miss me, but this had just come up.

I acted as if I fell for it. Carolyn III didn't care that much for her sisters. She was going visiting I was sure, but I suspected her visit consisted of extending her weekend with her lover.

I gave Carolyn III time to clear out Monday and figured I had 24 hours. First things first, I retrieved the five spy cams I had purchased and concealed around the house the previous Thursday morning.

My clothes were not a problem. Three garbage bags and a couple of wardrobe boxes from U-Haul held everything. My tools in the garage rolled easily up the U-Haul ramp still in their rolling stacked toolbox without having to pack them. I had a couple of dayworkers load the gun safe and the heavy things.

I would need a couch, and a recliner, and the big screen, the smaller kitchen table in the mudroom, three chairs and my desk and files, a few personal photos. I took the bed from the extra bedroom—I had no use for the king bed in the master bedroom that my wife had defiled.

Those were all loaded by noon. I thought it funny how one life of decades could fit inside a 32-foot U-Haul and be loaded within a few hours. The living room looked empty but going through the rest of the house at first glance one would never know that I was not still living there.

My friend Allen Maxey drove the U-Haul to my old family place in the mountains. It was the name of my parent's, thank God, and the renters had vacated the old house a couple of months earlier. I had a lot of repairs to do before it was rent-able again that I had been putting off, and again—circumstances worked in my favor.

I stopped by our bank on the way out of Woodstock and closed out all the joint accounts, canceled all the credit cards that I could, and just for good measure canceled her cell phone, the power, water, and sewer and every other utility and service I could remember.

Carolyn could get them all turned back on easily, I knew, but then again at least she would have to go to the inconvenience of doing so.

I stood in the driveway of the house we had both so excitedly discovered and worried together for the loan approval and the final closing. It had been my home until I left for my supposed trip to Ohio. Now it was only a cold building housing a woman I no longer wanted and a life I could no longer lead.

I fought the impulse to spread gasoline throughout the house, turn on the gas and strike a match. I considered it, but despite my pain and wrath, decided against it. Too much downside in the long term.

I recalled reading about one husband in a similar situation who bulldozed his house, but he was in the contracting business and had the dozer—and had time to secure the permit to do so. I had neither time, a permit, nor a bulldozer. Instead, I said, "goodbye," and "Fuck it" to that life and turned North toward the Carolina border and my old home that would now become my new home.

By dark that same night, I was in the mountains, unloaded in my old house, a bevy of boxes spread in the different rooms, and I sat in the dining room, replaying the footage from the hidden cams. I could only watch a few minutes before breaking down in sobs, but I was determined to see it all, to hear everything said. Much of it I did not want to hear, but my wanting did not change the reality.

Hearing your wife tell another man that she loves him is something no husband should ever have to hear. I broke for another drink and fought off another sobbing fit when my cell rang. The number seemed familiar, my old area code, but I didn't recognize it. The caller's name was restricted. That was when I realized it was the number of her Apple phone.

I was not through with viewing the footage—but I had seen enough that I knew there was no way I could salvage my marriage, nor did I want to.

"Max, we've been robbed," she said. "I've called the police. The TV's gone, and the couch, and on top of that today my credit card didn't work and…" It was at that moment I think she realized she was calling on the Apple phone she was not supposed to own, and that maybe she had not been robbed. She went silent.

"Yes, we've been robbed," I said. "You have robbed me, yourself, and our children of a happy home, a normal childhood, and the comfort and bliss of a faithful marriage."

"No, Max. It's not like that. I love you. I didn't mean…" I hung up the phone. That was the last civil thing she ever said to me.

The lawyer served divorce papers a week later, along with copies of the spycam video. She didn't contest much at first. Her new lover moved right in. In Georgia, the divorce took 30 days to finalize.

I was fine with that, willing to let things alone and go on with my life until she went back before a judge, lied and claimed I had beat my own kids. The female judge agreed with no proof other than my wife's word, and I was put on restricted visitation.

I see my kids as much as the court will allow, but at my request, her sister handles the transfers, so I do not have to see my ex-wife.

Her sister knows better than to mention Carolyn's name to me on the three or four times a year I am allowed the privilege of supervised visitation. For their own sakes, I did not try to explain to them what a lying cheating worthless tramp their mother is. I will wait until they are old enough to understand, although I have the feeling in the back of my mind that they will discover how their mother is long before that time.

I pray that my daughter will not follow her mother's example.

The fallout from the crash of my marriage with Carolyn III began what became almost a ritual from my friends. Whenever I would be seen with any female, they would quickly be asking, "Her name's not Carolyn is it?"

It was not as if I went celibate, although for six months after I didn't even think about another woman. I have a small circle of close friends, all married, and I discovered something about married friends who have an unmarried single friend in their circle. The unmarried man is out of balance in their world.

Men should have a woman in their way of thinking. A man without a woman might put weird ideas in the heads of the married men. An unmarried man in their circle makes the wives uncomfortable. So the remedy is to get the unmarried man remarried again as quickly as possible to return their world back to the proper balance.

Each couple in my circle knew someone they thought would be perfect for me. They were not around when I would go out with their recommended friend and be subject to a couple of hours of listening to what a low-rent son-of-a-bitch their ex-husband had been. I'd try for two or three dates just to appease my friends and give them time to let up on me—but not one date clicked. Several of my dates were nice women. A few would make a great mate for someone else, but not for me.

One overriding fact that I would not admit to anyone except myself, and only then late at night in the dark with far too much to drink was none of the arranged dates were Carolyn, not Carolyn I, not Carolyn II, or Carolyn III. At the same time, deep within me, I wanted a manifestation of the Carolyn of my imagination, but I knew I had to be through with Carolyns for my own battered sanity.

Two years after the divorce I received a Christmas card, one of those with five or six photos on one side of a thick card. There were my two kids, my ex-wife, and her lover. She was holding a new baby in her arms. It was not Christmas wishes. She wanted to rub my nose in it. I threw the card in the trash.

Chapter 24

After my marriage to Carolyn III disintegrated, it changed me. I learned to stay skinny on household gear. I had taken a minimalist approach to home furnishings and material things. Clearing out what I needed for Carolyn McMasters and I to disappear from Huntington for a while did not take long. Material things mean little to me, a place to sit, a place to sleep, paper plates from the big box store eliminated a lot of dishwashing.

All I needed for the road was a toilet kit, a few changes of clothes, and a laptop with the pictures that formed the history of my life all digitized in a portable hard drive.

I could fit everything important to my life in the trunk of a car. Burn my house down and I could furnish it again for a few thousand dollars and would have lost nothing important. I was ready to leave in the morning, and I returned to the Patterson's chalet. I did not want to leave Carolyn McMasters alone too long.

I loaded my essentials, inspired by suspecting there could soon be unsavory characters headed in my direction. I kept a loaded pistol holstered on my hip as I did my loadout.

***

With my essentials in my SUV, I still had non-essentials things I needed to secure before we bugged out. I called on friends. Allen, the one man in the world who always had my back, rented a secure storage in his name but with my name on the card too, for later access. I gave him a quick rundown of what was happening and why I needed his help. He was all in. He stopped by Walmart and purchased their best smartphone burner with 2000 minutes. Through my laptop, I added my contact list and was back in business for sales.

What I sought was not a plan of action, although I needed one—but nothing was coming to mind. I needed time to get out of the immediate danger and thus have time to form a plan.

Taking a cue from Carolyn McMasters on the way to the chalet, I stopped by the truck stop and gave my Samsung to one Eddie Armstrong. Eddie's of the local boys who hated school but loves driving, so he drives for a snack cake company on cross country truck runs. I told him to use the phone all he wanted until the end of the month, just stay away from kiddie porn. I didn't want an account with my name associated with anything like that.

He was heading to upstate New York via Buffalo. I suggested he toss the phone into the Niagara. He said he would.

And thus divested of most of the traceable links to my current life, I spent an hour on the burner phone. The hour spent calling yielded no luck or even a good contact for a sword sale.

Chapter 25

The Biscuit Barn on the four-lane approaching Huntington makes legendary breakfasts. I called ahead for two King plates and picked them up to avoid the line and the typical half-hour wait. Placing the meals in a cooler to keep them hot, I was knocking on the chalet door in minutes.

Carolyn came to the door in a robe, her hair wet and a towel in her hand. She looked more beautiful than she did made up, I thought.

"I hope I'm not too early. I brought breakfast." Street bounded past me, 56 pounds of eager Lab, sniffing and wagging his tail, licking the hand she extended.

"Oh aren't you a pretty thing," she said, rubbing behind her ears. "Yours?"

"Yeah, this is Street."

"Pleased to meet you, Street," she said. As if on cue Street raised a paw for a shake.

"Wow, you teach him to do that?" I nodded. Street could do a lot more than a shake. He is a smart dog.

"Actually, that's the first time I've ever seen him react like that. Dogs have a sense about people you know."

Carolyn looked away. "Damn, I can even fool a dog. I must be a better actress than I thought."

"No, you can't," I said. Holding up the bag I reminded, "Breakfast?"

"Thank God. I'm famished. I didn't sleep much last night."

She invited me in. The robe fell open and I saw she was wearing a long flannel nightgown. Carolyn did not miss my glance.

"You were expecting something sheer and lacy?"

"Only hoping," I said. Street went to the area rug at the edge of the kitchen and curled up as if he had laid there for years.

"Sorry. Not your typical sexy California girl. Especially, with what is going on."

"What do you mean?"

"Come here." She said, pointing toward the dining room table. "I would have preferred to be sipping my coffee enjoying this beautiful view, but I made the mistake of checking on something." She sat at the table in front of an open laptop a laptop. I set the boxes of food on the counter. "Watch," she said.

On the screen were scenes from surveillance cameras. "I had these installed a while back. I can access them through the net," she said.

The time stamp said it was 3:30 a.m. California time. 6:30 here. Two and a half hours ago. The exterior shot showed three men at the door. I recognized it as Carolyn's massive wood front door. As we watched the video two of the men drew pistols and the third broke the door in with a large ram, following the front two who rushed through the door, one low, one high. The third man dropped the ram, drew a pistol of his own and followed the other two inside.

"They look like the same men who were outside my house when I left," she said. "They must have waited for it to be dark and likely for everyone to be asleep to return."

It reminded me of a SWAT assault as we watched the intrusion via the various security cameras. The three coursed through the house room by room, one looking right, one left, one center when they rushed in, guns drawn and ready to shoot, clearing the house. Once they realized the house was empty, they turned on the lights and began searching the house, opening closets, and breaking down the locked door to the room that housed the large gun safe.

One of the men placed a cell phone call when he came to the huge safe. In the other room, the taller of the three carefully went through the papers of Carolyn's desk, piece by piece, while the third guarded the front door.

"When did you start watching this?"

"I checked it a half-hour ago. I called the Santa Barbara police as soon as I saw what was happening."

"Do they arrive?"

"Just watch." Her voice was shaky. Carolyn fast-forwarded for 30 minutes, still showing the men rifling through her home. They were thorough, and as they finished their search, one remained at the door as a sentry while the other two waited in the safe room. One of them noticed the large photo of Carolyn on the wall and grabbed his crotch, nudging his companion and making an obscene remark in Spanish.

"Asshole," Carolyn said to the screen.

A fourth person arrived, a chubby Latino carrying a large toolbox, and he was escorted to the safe room. He opened the toolbox, flipped through a manual, and compared the safe to the ones shown in the book. He read a minute longer before withdrawing a battery-powered drill, drilling a half dozen holes into the safe door.

Fifteen minutes of effort later he nodded, turned the dial and the safe door opened. Carolyn snickered. "Sorry," she said. "Looks like someone cleaned it out earlier."

The disappointment showed on the faces of the men, and their heads turned in unison and they moved to the living room as they heard the sentry at the door give an alert. With guns drawn, they flanked the door.

From the outside camera we could see two police officers in uniform approaching the door, guns holstered.

They never stood a chance. The four men filled the doorway; two squatted down, two standing, bracing against the door frame for accuracy and they opened on the two officers. It did not last but a few seconds. Both officers went down immediately. Head shots and upper thighs. No body armor protected them there.

"Oh shit," I screamed helpless as I watched the murder of two men. "What the hell!"

"I know," Carolyn said. As we continued to watch in stunned shock, the taller man stepped to each officer and added another shot to their heads. A coup de grace.

The officers' bodies were drug into the house, and the four men calmly walked to their vans and drove away, the lights of the police car still flashing blue against the white side of the vans as they drove away.

"Did you…"

"Yes, I called the police the minute I saw what happened. I described the vans. Look, they have the tags covered." She pointed to the video. She was right. "I've copied the video and emailed it to the police department. That's all I can do."

"You did good," I said. "That is exactly what you should have done."

"If I had not left yesterday, I would have still been home."

"But you did leave."

"Yes, I did. Now what?"

"I'm not sure," I said. "They knew the officers might be wearing body armor, they shot for the head and thighs. You saw how they entered the house. Professionals."

"I'm scared," Carolyn said, "I'm really scared," breaking into tears and reaching for me. I pulled her close and pressed her against me. Other than the initial handshake it was the first time we touched. I tried my best to comfort her, patting her shoulder.

"Don't worry. It will be all right," I said, wrapping my arm around her shoulders and rubbing softly, even though at that moment I couldn't think of what we could do to stop what was coming—except run.

Chapter 26

Finally, Carolyn's sobs lessened, and she looked up with red puffy eyes, almost in a whimper said, "I need coffee."

I poured her a cup, set the Styrofoam box from the Biscuit Barn in front of her. "Eat. You need to keep your strength up."

"I'm a nervous eater anyway—that's another reason I never made it acting, I was always about 10 pounds heavier than the director wanted, and TV makes you look 10 pounds more than you really are. I got down to the weight they wanted a few times, but I couldn't keep it off."

"You?"

"They like really skinny. I like to eat too much."

"Then eat." Carolyn dove in the food hesitantly at first, then faster.

"Damn, this is pretty good," she said with her mouth full. She emptied her coffee before I finished my meal, but I stopped, refilled her coffee and set it back on the table with a bottle of Jameson's from the bar. "Coffee from the old country," I said. She nodded, and I added the Jamie to the coffee.

Carolyn said nothing else until she finished wolfing down the breakfast. It was interesting watching a woman who a few days earlier greeted me as an aloof sophisticate now devouring a breakfast as if she had not eaten for days. She was a chameleon. When she finished, she stood, carried the box to the trash and refilled her coffee, topping it off with more Jamie, pausing to walk over to Street and pat his raised head. He pressed his head against her hand as she rubbed him.

Carolyn walked past me through the living room out on the deck that boasted seven ranges of mountains from the swing in which she took a seat, each range a different hue of blue, like massive ocean waves. I took my coffee and sat beside her, the faint scent of pine in air. Street followed us out, sitting at her feet.

"This is crazy, a fucking nightmare, and I started it. I should have never told my brother. I am having a nightmare, right?" She looked up at me. "I'm not hiding out in some little mountain town hidden out by a man I barely know. This is not real, is it?"

"Unfortunately, it is reality," I said. "I do not think the video was staged. We have to think this through."

"I have to trust you," Carolyn said. "And I don't trust anyone. I learned that a long time ago. Tell me why I should trust you, Max Kugar. Make me comfortable with you. Please." There was no arrogance that I had seen in California in her plea.

"I can't do that, you have to figure that out for yourself," I said. "I like to think I'm one of the good guys, but everyone does. Al Capone beat two men to death with a ball bat and said later he had done nothing wrong; it was only business."

"Damn, that sure helped," she wisecracked.

"Sorry. I don't know what to say. You checked me out on background. Anything there that would make you ill at ease?"

"No, not really," Carolyn said. "If there had been, I would never have contacted you."

"That's a start then."

"What did you find about me?" Carolyn asked. "I know you checked; I got a couple of alerts from my privacy program."

"From what I could read and what I observed since we met, you always were deferred to because you have always been prettier than most of the other women around you. You got used to it and went to California planning to make it big and something went wrong once you got there.

"You settled in with a man who you thought had some promise and could help promote you, with whom you felt a connection, and somewhere along the line he veered off into drugs and it did him in. There's not a lot about you after his death."

"I loved him. He built me up after I realized that I was not going to be a success as an actor. He helped me through those head games and the disappointment, and I loved him for that. He was so nice when we first met, but he changed. I was living with a stranger at the end—and the way he went out, overdosing with two bimbettes in a run-down bungalow—I saw it coming but didn't face it. I was in a tailspin of my own and went a little crazy when he died.

"He had borrowed against everything we owned. In Santa Barbara, I am in hock up to my eyeballs. I spent a year sitting on my deck staring out at the ocean and keeping a drink in my hand. The money's gone. It is only a matter of a few payments before the bank takes it back.

"That was why I even considered selling the sword. I knew there would be a lot of shit that would come with trying to sell the sword—I just never imagined it would come to this."

"You don't think we can give your brother the sword and all this go away?" I said.

"No. He and the people he works with do not believe in loose ends. Us even knowing the sword exists would condemn us after what he said. He is risking everything on this Japanese deal."

"Well there is one option we have not considered," I said.

"What's that?"

"Kill them all. First."

***

Carolyn sat a long time without speaking and then agreed. "Yes. That might work."

"You would be OK with that?" I asked.

"At the moment, yes. Live and let live I believe, but anyone trying to kill me, it will be only if I do not get them first."

"You say that now. Nothing gets more serious in this life than taking the life of another human being, no matter how they might deserve it or bring it on themselves. You ever killed anything?" I asked.

"Not knowingly."

"Ever fired a gun?"

"No. Grandad tried to get me to, but I refused, he never pushed it."

"Come on," I said, going to my truck, reaching behind the seat and pulling out a padded case, unzipping it and withdrawing a six-inch barrel Smith & Wesson .357 Magnum, three speed loaders and a box of shells. Following my instructions, Carolyn loaded six rounds. "Now shoot," I said.

"At what?"

"Doesn't matter. I just want to you get the feel of the gun, to know what the recoil is like. We will work on the accuracy later." I handed her the earmuffs and she squeezed off the six rounds just as I had instructed. By the third cylinder of cartridges, she was within the chest area of a man-sized target at 25 yards. "That's close enough for now. You are a good student. I'm going to leave this one with you. Load it, and do not pull it and try to scare someone—only pull it if you are prepared to shoot. When the person threatening your life first sees it, the pistol should be spitting fire and lead. Pulling a gun has consequences, and if the situation has deteriorated to the point you are forced to draw your pistol, the rule is the person you do not want dying is yourself. For that to happen you must put the other person down and not attempt to threaten with the gun. You shoot. Understand?" She nodded.

"I'm going to make a run into town. I'll be back before dark if I can. If not, I will stop at the end of the drive and beep the horn twice. Don't shoot me."

I saw the fear rise again. She did not want to be alone. "You will be all right." I pointed to the gaps at the foot of the hill. "You see anyone, and I mean anyone but me coming up that hill, take the pistol and ammunition and head up the hill behind the storage building. The trail goes into the laurel there. Once on top, the trail splits. Take the left and I will meet you at the small waterfall. You can hide in the laurel there and no one will see you. Got it?" Carolyn nodded.

"I'll leave Street here," I said. "He would be useless in attacking anyone, but no one will be able to sneak up on you without him barking. Pay attention to his body language."

"Thanks. I'll enjoy the company," she said. "Street? That's a strange name for a dog."

"Actually it's Longstreet, Robert E. Lee's "old warhorse" they called him."

"You named a dog after a Civil War general?" She squinted and wrinkled up her nose as she did. She didn't understand.

"What could be any better? Besides, it suits him." Street started wagging his tail when he saw me looking at him. Carolyn gave me an eye roll.

"I have a couple of stops to make but I'll be back soon. Don't throw a tennis ball to him unless you plan to be doing it for a while—and the ball will get slobbery. He's obsessive when it comes to tennis balls."

"Really?" Carolyn said, a hint of excitement in her eyes.

"They're in a basket on top of the fridge," I said. "The Patterson's have a blond lab themselves and always keep their balls there."

At the bottom of the hill, I glanced up back at the chalet. Through the trees, I could see Carolyn with her hair blowing in the wind, gleefully throwing the bright tennis ball and Street in full flight bounding after it, his tail wagging as he brought it back to for another throw. Street was in heaven. I envied him at that moment.

Chapter 27

I was buzzed through by the receptionist sitting behind a thick sheet of yellowing scratched plexiglass with a small curved hole at the bottom to slide things through, with a cardboard box pressed against the hole. She was sweating, and a box fan was on the desk behind her. She buzzed me through, and I knocked on the sheriff's door. "Come in," was the brusque reply. "Max, how the hell are you?"

Oconoluftee County Sheriff Calvin Gray pushed up with his shoulders as if he was doing a push-up and waddled around his old wood desk and gave me an embrace. Despite his bulk, his uniform was spotless, as was his office. On his wall was a framed photo of him with an M-16 and the Vietnamese jungle behind him. There were two Viet-Cong bodies in front of him, like hunting trophies.

Calvin was past retirement age, but his fairness and reputation meant the job was his for as long as he wanted to remain Sheriff.

He no longer had the build he had in Vietnam, but as a couple of would-be bank robbers had discovered the year before, he still had the resolve, and the accuracy.

Calvin answered the silent alarm at the bank and pulled up while they were still inside, his rifle up and aimed at the door when they burst through into the daylight. They made two massive mistakes. They did not stop when Calvin ordered "freeze" in his best command voice—and they both raised their pistols to the sound of his voice.

The gunfight lasted as long as it takes to squeeze off four .223 rounds from a semi-automatic AR. It would be much quicker now after I had assisted the department.

"Good, Sheriff, Good. How are those rifles holding up?"

"Great, I am grateful for you arranging it."

"My pleasure."

"What can I do you for?" Calvin grinned. I was the fair-haired child around the county sheriff's department. As a kid, I recalled the time they moved the cash from the old bank to the new bank building across the street, and in one of the photos, a heavy-set deputy was guarding the transfer with an old M3 submachine gun commonly known as a Grease Gun held at port arms.

I mentioned that recollection to one of my contacts, a Class 3 firearms dealer, in casual conversation.

"If they still have that gun, I can give them a hell of a swap for some new Colt M4 Carbines, full auto." He said.

They still had it, and in one brief exchange, my mountain county had become the most heavily armed force in that part of the state.

"How are things? Casino brought more trouble with it?" I asked. An Indian casino had been built on a section of tribal land in the county shortly after Calvin took office for his most recent term.

"Nothing we haven't been able to handle—but we have been catching an increased number of Mexicans coming in with drugs. I'm not sure how organized it is, but they do know there is a market here through the casino. We're trying to keep our eyes open."

"I had heard that," I said, and got right to the point of my meeting. "I also got wind from a friend down in Texas that the cartels are sending some sicarios to take out some competition. No way to prove anything and he didn't want his name attached, but something he overheard, one of the known guys in a bar in Cuidad Acuna asking where the hell Huntington, North Carolina was."

"No shit?" Calvin said, leaned forward and seeing I wasn't smiling knew it wasn't a joke. He leaned back. "Let the motherfuckers come. We've got the firepower thanks to you."

"Just hoping you could get the boys to open their eyes a little wider. Much less of a storm if you see it coming. And I'm going out of town for a few days. If anyone sees anyone around my place, no one is supposed to be there."

"Woman involved Max?" He grinned.

"Maybe," I teased.

"Her name is not Carolyn is it?" Damn, I thought, everyone in town is in on the taunt.

"You know me better than that, Sheriff."

"Have a good trip and fuck her once for me," he smiled. "Thanks for the tip," Calvin said.

"Not that kind of a trip Sheriff," I said.

Chapter 28

I wasn't sure if Carolyn had mentioned my name to her brother, but once he secured her phone records and sorted out that she was not carrying her cell, it would not take a genius to determine who I was, or where to find me if I hung around here. The text messages and a reverse phone directory would pinpoint me.

I figured we might have a day or two, but the reality of hanging around there wasn't really an option.

The nice thing about my line of work is customers and clients are widespread and not prone to get too nosy if you show up in town unannounced. There were places we could go—but traveling takes money.

The bank wasn't too happy when I asked for half my ready cash, all 15 grand of it. I had to fill out a pile of paperwork, but I left with it in a leather dispatch case. I stopped at my warehouse and cleaned out my small stash of trading cash in the safe of another five grand, a box of silver dollars, and a half-dozen Krugerrands.

Everything else of value was in my gun safe, and Dex at the gun shop was happy to give me some space in his back to store it for the cash payment I gave him. I wasn't leaving a paper trail. The piano movers had the safe in his shop within two hours. I knew he had the best alarm system within 40 miles. He promised to let me know if anyone came around asking about me.

I retained my 12-gauge riot gun, an AR15 with a collapsible stock, the same frame in a .308, Three Glocks, a 22, 43, and 27; an airweight S&W J-frame Bodyguard .38. The pistols fit in the dispatch case except for the 43 single stack 9mm that I put in a cross draw belt holster on my left side, covered by a long sweatshirt. Everything else fit nicely in the canvas duffel along with full magazines and ammo.

It was not much of an arsenal for war, and too many for a car trip—but it was better to hump the guns around than to need one and not have it close at hand.

***

When I returned to the chalet everything was quiet. The lights were off inside. I unlocked the door. Carolyn was leaned back in the recliner dozing and Street, all full-grown lab of him, was curled up on her lap. There was as much dog as there was woman in the chair.

I called Street to me, and he raised his head but did not move. "He likes me," she smiled without opening her eyes. "And I like him. We've bonded." She moved, and Street jumped off as she stood. Carolyn had changed into jeans and a dark blue tank top with a zip-up hoodie over that. She had spent some time on her hair and had applied light make-up with no jewelry. She gleamed. Her face was one that jewelry on her body would only serve as a distraction.

I'm human and had not missed her beauty—and it was taking all my concentration to not be distracted by it. We had to focus on more important things—like staying alive.

"OK, what have you come up with?" Carolyn asked.

"Have you ever thought about hiking the Appalachian Trail?" I asked.

"When do we leave?"

"How soon can you pack?"

"Five minutes. But I don't have any hiking gear."

"Let me worry about that. Pack everything, leave nothing to tie you to here," I said. We placed her two hastily packed bags in the back of my SUV.

***

As I wound down the gravel driveway from the Patterson's chalet, at a switchback curve I saw a scratched black truck half concealed in the brush. I stopped and got out, taking two steps toward the truck.

"Vernon?" I said. "Vernon Crump?"

"Yo," I heard a voice, and turning to the rustle in the brush I saw a tall skinny man with faded camo hanging off his body emerge, a 12-gauge pump shotgun cradled in the crook of his arm. He had a silly grin on his face as if he had been caught flattening someone's tires.

"What are you doing here? It's not hunting season."

"I know," Vernon said, still with the silly smile. "I bumped into Allen. He suggested that making sure no strangers were coming and going through here might be a help. I should have known there was a pretty woman involved."

"So, you thought I might need some help?" I asked.

"Didn't think it would hurt," he said. "Besides, Irene was getting on my nerves with those crappy TV shows she wants me to watch with her. Hell, I have to wait until she goes shopping before I can even consider turning on the Outdoor Channel."

"Well, I do appreciate the consideration. Only a friend would do that. How long you been out here?" I asked.

"A while," was Vernon's only answer. I knew that was as specific as he would get. "Well again, thanks, but you can go on home now, I'm going out of town. Already locked the place up."

"No problem," Vernon said. "You go on out, I'll lock the gate behind you."

I paused. "I locked the gate when I went out, how did you get in here?" Vernon just grinned.

"There are ways," he said. He held up a small leather kit that I recognized as a lock picking set.

"Your abilities never surprise me," I said.

"Jack of all trades."

"And the master of none," I tossed back. I stepped forward and shook his hand. "I'll see you later," I said.

"Be sure that you do," he cautioned. I climbed back into the Expedition and put it in gear.

"Who was that?" Carolyn asked.

"Vernon. A friend."

"What was he doing there?"

"Watching over us, like a mother hen," I said.

"How long was he out there, I never saw anything there."

"You wouldn't unless he wanted you to see him," I said. "He spends more time outdoors than he does indoors. Always has. I would not be surprised if he had been there most of the night."

"That would take a friend," Carolyn said.

"Yes, it would. We go back." I said.

"How far?" she asked.

"Far enough."

***

Before we left town, I drove to Terry's, the kid that helps me with odd jobs and handles all the upkeep on my website. After my move home, I had given up finding anyone in Huntington with the ability to maintain a modern website and was complaining about it at the barber shop while I waited for a haircut.

Another man waiting introduced himself as the math teacher at Huntington High and said he had a student who was amazing in that kind of thing. That kid was Terry. He introduced us.

We stopped in the gravel driveway of his parent's yellow double-wide manufactured home. "Let me see your driver's license," I said to Carolyn. "And come on."

Carolyn didn't question me, digging through her brown bucket-size purse, removing it from her checkbook folder and handing me the license. "Don't look at my license photo," she said. "It's awful."

"Everyone says that," I answered. She followed me down the gravel path and up the narrow wood steps with green mold on the corners to the screen door of the porch.

Terry came onto the porch and did the expected double take on Carolyn, and she beamed at the stare. She enjoys that attention I realized, and for a geek like Terry, this was a momentous occasion. I explained what we needed.

Inside Terry led us to the dining room, where he took two photos of each of us against the white dining room wall. Carolyn shucked off the hoodie and I noticed a rose tattooed on her back peeking out from under the left strap of her tank. She pulled her hoodie back on immediately. "Cold in here," she said. I handed him the two licenses. "Do as good as you can," I said.

"I'll try," he grinned. "What if you get stopped in the meantime?"

"I have a duplicate. I thought I lost my wallet last year, turned it in and they replaced the license, then I found the wallet."

"Nice," Terry said. "I had not thought of that. I'll use it."

Back in the SUV Carolyn asked, "What was that about? Hell, he doesn't look old enough to drive."

"He's 18 actually. Terry is a good kid with a bad complexion. He does work for me sometimes. Computer geek, but he makes extra money doing fake ID for his classmates. He's very good at it."

"We are having fake ID's made?"

"You have a better idea?" I ask.

"Couldn't hurt," Carolyn said.

We passed the drive going to the Patterson's chalet on the way out, and we could see it in the distance, like a gingerbread house atop a rounded cake with green fluffy icing. The opening in between the two oaks framed the view. She looked up at the chalet through the gap in the trees. "It was peaceful there, I was beginning to like it," Carolyn said. "This is the first time I've ever spent time in a place like this. It's beautiful."

"It is that," I said, "But this is a small town. A lot here depends on which political party you register as a member of—those are public record. You want a local county job now you have to be registered as a Democrat."

"What are you?" she asked.

"Independent," I said, although now when you register you can no longer be an independent but 'unaffiliated.'"

"I could have called that one," Carolyn said. As we drove out of town she asked, "One thing I do not understand, why do all these real estate people have their photos on their billboards, if they were selling homes I would think they would show an upscale home in their listings."

"I asked one of my broker friends the same thing," I said. "He said it was ego and nothing more."

Carolyn looked up at a billboard with an unattractive old man grinning a dark tooth smile. "I think some of them might do well if they kept their faces off their billboards. Still, it is so beautiful here."

"On the surface, there are a lot of beautiful places in this country, each with their own special flair. I like the swamps of Louisiana, the Mississippi Delta, the desert around Soccoro, New Mexico, Yosemite is one of the prettiest places I've ever been in my life."

"I like Yosemite too," Carolyn said. "My late husband and I went there a couple of times." She paused, "We hiked then. Are you serious about hiking the Appalachian Trail?"

"Think about it, the perfect place to blend in, 2000 miles of possible places we could be."

"Makes sense to me. It's been a while though. You'll have to start off slow. I'm out of shape."

***

We were driving south toward Atlanta before she noticed. "Didn't we come up this way the other night?"

"Yes."

"Why are we going back? Isn't this past the beginning of the Appalachian Trail? We're not near Springer Mountain."

"Something like that. We have to gear up." I was impressed. She could read a map and had some situational awareness. I said nothing else, and she did not question further. At 11:30 I was feeling my first hunger pang. "Ready for some lunch?" I asked, "Something ethnic?"

"Ethnic? Sure. What you have in mind, Thai? Indian? Or?" I turned my blinker and pulled into the parking lot of a weathered clapboard building capped with a large pink neon pig. A plume of smoke was rising from a small outbuilding with a huge exhaust fan extruding from its side. The oak smoke aroma hit before we even opened a door.

"Southern ethnic, Barbeque," I said. "You cannot get real barbeque outside the South, and it has to be dead pig." She wrinkled up her nose without laughing.

I ordered a rib sampler platter for her and a large sandwich with mustard slaw for myself through the drive-through. I didn't want to stay anywhere too long at the moment, and that included a sit-down in a restaurant.

"My God, I had no idea barbeque could taste like this," she said three minutes later, cramming the ribs in her mouth and licking the sauce off her fingers as I continued driving South.

"You have the dry rub," I said pointing, "Memphis claims that. The vinegar base is eastern Carolina, and the thick red is molasses based sweet sauce is found a lot of places." I laughed at the mess she was making with her hands dipping in the sauce and how she had to wipe her hands with the steadily decreasing tall stack of napkins as she did.

"OK, enough games," she said. "We are in this together, where are we going?"

"When are you going to tell me where the sword is?"

"I'm not until you get me a buyer."

"Well sit back and enjoy the ride Ma'am," I smiled. "Life can be full of surprises."

By the time she had finished her lunch, we were pulling into the parking lot of the big green Bass Pro Shop.

"I get it now, backpacking supplies," she said.

"Something like that. We'll equip here and at Cabelas up the road. You still have your credit cards?"

"I do."

"Max them out here. This is the last time you will use them. Too easy to trace," I said.

I had a list, and I wanted to keep her close. We each had a buggy that was soon heaping: backpacks, good Keltys; two backpacking tents, lightweight cooking utensils, a lightweight stove, lights, freeze dried food, a couple of weeks' worth, canteens, and new hiking shoes, heavy duty socks, a variety of convertible pants with zip off legs making them shorts and quick dry tops.

Carolyn was a quick shopper. It didn't take her long to make up her mind, but then again it is hard to be stylish with backpacking gear. "I love spending money," she said. "Even my own. Looks like we have everything we need."

"Everything except different underwear," I laughed. "No room for thongs on the trail."

"No problem," Carolyn shot back. "I rarely wear underwear unless it is a thong, and never bras. I read the "Dressed to Kill" book, there's some serious research that says they are unhealthy." She saw my puzzled look, opening her zip-up hoodie to reveal her thin and tight tank top and her obvious lack of a bra. I stared a second too long, I guess. "Oh hell, don't tell me you haven't noticed?"

I shook my head no. "Damn, you are focused," she said shaking her head.

"No objection to the theory though."

"It's good to see you're acting a little human," Carolyn said.

"I'm human. But I will try to be more human. How's that?"

"I would have not known it by the way you've acted since I first met you. You're almost like a robot. It is like you are thinking about something else all the time."

"I like to think ahead."

"It's OK to think in the present sometimes too." She said. I looked at her and she held the gaze a second too long in my direction. I kept a poker face, but I recognized the game. A beautiful woman used to turning heads gets curious when a man doesn't pay attention. Something had to be wrong with him...or her, and the doubting begins.

Of course, the exceptions to that rule is when a man is older or fat. They are invisible to pretty women by nature.

***

With our gear stowed in the Expedition, Carolyn was silent for a while, then brought up Vernon. "Your friend back there, the one in the bushes, what caused him to be out there? Did you ask him to guard us?"

"No. He said he bumped into Allen, told him I was trying to lay low, and Vernon figured the rest out. He took it on himself to come out to be on guard."

"Why would he do that without prompting?" She asked.

"Instinct, from him," I said. "We grew up together, like brothers. He's the only person I know who can look at a bear track and tell you how many hours old it is and in which direction the bear is headed. He just has a sense like that."

"Still, he felt like you needed overseeing. Why?"

"Because there is a woman involved. He knows very well how that can distract a man."

"So, I am distracting you?" Carolyn said, a knowing smile of achievement crossing her face.

"To some extent."

"And Kit Carson back there, he knows how distracted you can get around women?"

"He knows, he's a man. He's been there too. Most of us have."

"Oh OK," Carolyn said, her ego satisfied that she had my attention.

***

For Vernon it was a clearer lesson. During his senior year in high school he had a six-month infatuation with a freshman cheerleader, Sallie March. Her Uncle Marsh married my Aunt, so we were always together at family reunions, but no blood relation. Vernon fell in love with her. When left to go to middle Tennessee to work in a car factory, she started dating the fullback on the football team.

Whenever I would bump into Vernon, when we happened to be back home in Huntington at the same time, he would always ask if I had seen Sallie. He was despondent when she married the fullback shortly after graduation.

It was fated that five years later I saw Vernon in the paint department of Wal-Mart, and as usual, he asked about Sallie. My response was different this time.

"Yes, she was at the family reunion this past weekend, and she asked about you," I said.

Vernon straightened to attention, a strange thing for him because he was usually in an Ichabod Crain slump. "She did?"

"Yeah, and I told her that you asked about her at times too, so she scribbled down her phone number on the back of my business card. Here it is." I reached for my wallet and handed him the card, with a caution. "Sallie is separated from her husband, and if you call her and take her out whatever you may do, under no circumstances take her back to her house. Her husband is fighting the divorce and is trying to intimidate anyone who tries to date her."

"Well..." Vernon started to say but I interrupted.

"And he is big and mean, one of those Crutchfields from Little Creek, 'Big Bob' they call him." Vernon nodded and stepped away, reaching for his cell phone as he headed toward the door. I knew who he was calling.

Later that night I was at my Mom and Dad's house, they had gone out of town to his Navy destroyer crew reunion, and I heard a knock at the door. I opened it and there stood Vernon, bruised, bloodied with a deep purple spot on his cheekbone, a busted lip, buck naked except for a pair of athletic shoes. "What the fuck?" I said as he stood on the porch leaning on the porch rocker. Then it hit me. "You took her back to her house, didn't you?"

Vernon nodded. Then the stench hit me. He had specks of brown gunk on his lower legs. "Get me a wet towel," he said. "He actually did kick the shit out of me."

***

Thirty minutes later after a shower and what almost would be considered an alcohol bath, Vernon was decked out in a pair of my Dad's overalls and a dark tee, explaining what happened. His telling me the story was the price for providing the means for the clean-up.

Vernon had called Sallie and indeed she did want to see him, recalling the old times they had spent romping in the cabin of her Dad's boat, rarely used and out of site in the boathouse.

The two of them had gone out for a drink, and at her invitation straight back to Sallie's house.

"We had our clothes off and were in the bed in seconds, it seemed like," Vernon said wistfully. "We had finished, she was lighting a cigarette when I saw the headlights from a car flash against the bedroom wall. Sallie raised up, looked out the window and said, 'Oh my God. It's him.' With that, she ran out of the room into the bathroom."

"And then what?" I asked.

"The only thing I could think of was whatever might happen I'd better get my shoes on, so I put them on, tied them quickly, and stepped out into the hall. The front door burst open, and in walks this mountain of a man that fills up the whole doorway. He's crying. And I freeze."

"Let me get this right," I said, holding back a snicker. "This distraught husband walks into his house to see a naked man in nothing but a pair of tennis shoes standing in his hall?"

"Pretty much," Vernon said, not smiling. "About this time Sallie bursts out of the bathroom in a bathrobe, runs toward him and she's crying too. As she's running, she is wailing, 'I'm sorry baby.' When she gets within reach, he gives her a right cross to the face and she goes down like she was poleaxed, blood spurting from her nose and going everywhere.

"He is between me and the door, so I have this faint hope of running toward him, dropping down to my knees, sliding around him on the floor because of the slick blood, jumping up on the other side of him and rushing out the door. At least outside I had running room."

"How did that work out," I asked.

"I did the run, slid down to the floor and came to a screeching halt right in front of his big cowboy boots, and he began to kick me. I thought I was going to die. You've heard of people kicking the shit out of someone, well he did. I couldn't help it. I was curled up in a ball and finally, Sallie got up and he turned back to her long enough to allow me to get up and run outside."

"So you got away?"

"Not quite," Vernon said. "I had left my car keys inside. I yelled for Sallie to throw me my keys. Her husband turns back to me and rushes me, but there is the car between us, so he circles left I go left, keeping the car between us, chasing me all over the yard, but I had on my running shoes and he was wearing those cowboy boots and I was able to stay ahead of him until Sallie threw me my keys. He turned back to her and I got in my car and drove here."

"Your clothes?"

"Still there."

"Your wallet?"

"Still there, going to stay there too. I can get another driver's license." I'm going back to Middle Tennessee till this all blows over. I'll be out of here first thing in the morning."

***

I didn't see Vernon for almost a year when on a visit to my parents they mentioned that he had moved back home and was dating Irene Misson. My folks knew where he was staying so I stopped by. We had a beer sitting on his porch and didn't speak for a while.

"I noticed you didn't ask about Sallie," I said.

"I know."

"That over?"

"Sallie went back to her husband; he took a job in Florida. I didn't dare come home until he had cleared out."

"Why not?" I asked.

"When I went back to Middle Tennessee, I got to thinking about my ass kicking so I called the florist and sent Sallie three dozen red roses."

"You what?" I laughed.

"I thought I'd show the son of a bitch," Vernon said.

"And how did that work out?"

"He got my cell number from somewhere and called fuming, he said he was going to come kill me, and for sure would kill me on sight if he caught me in Huntington or near his wife."

"You let that stop you?" I taunted with a smile.

"Hell yes," Vernon said, his eyes wide. "He was serious. I hear she has a kid with him now."

"And you are focused on Irene now?"

"Yeah, she's a lot safer," Vernon grinned.

Chapter 29

We drove back to the mountains where I stopped at Allen's car lot. It was small, a half dozen late model Ford pickups on the front row, a dozen older cars with "We tote the note" signs on the windshield in a graveled lot beyond the asphalt. A Chevy Impala rested inside the metal building where it was being detailed, mats clipped to the wall and a teenager eagerly vacuuming with a long brown hose.

Allen had six-foot-high American flags between each vehicle. It was impossible to miss.

Some of the newcomers once tried to protest the number of flags he flew at the zoning commission, but one of the local real estate brokers whispered in each of their ears and the motion was withdrawn instantly.

For a few hundred bucks rental, Allen was happy to furnish me with a nice ride and two dealer tags. I took two in case I needed to change my tag number.

Street went straight into Allen's office and curled up in his corner, he had been here before and Allen didn't mind taking care of Street. My lab had claimed that corner long before.

Carolyn gave him a nice petting and said goodbye while I unloaded Street's dish and a bag of food. She even kissed him on the muzzle.

I drove away in a used Ford Expedition customized with a metal sliding drawer in the back for securing firearms, formerly owned by a metro police department but repainted, the only indication of its earlier life the security drawer in the back.

I kept the single stack Glock 43 in my belt, the .40 cal Model 22 I put in the dash, three magazines for each, and stored the rest in the drawer. I traded the .357 to Carolyn for the .38 snubby and left the .357 with Allen.

I drove the older Expedition to Terry's and Carolyn followed in mine, still loaded with the backpacking gear. I directed her in backing the Expedition to his garage door.

Inside Terry handed me the two new ID's. "Here you go. Two North Carolina Driver's License. They should pass unless someone twists it in the light to see the hologram, I can't duplicate that," he said. "I've never seen anyone actually look for that anyway unless you're getting on a plane."

"Thanks," I said, glancing down to realize that he had used an Asheville address and our first names. The last name was the same, "Madison".

"Here you go, Mrs. Madison," I smiled as I handed the new ID to Carolyn.

"Oh crap, you mean we're acting married?"

"No one told me not to," Terry said. "I thought it made sense. You're together but you did not want to not stand out."

"Fair enough," I grinned, enjoying Carolyn's discomfort. "We don't have time to redo them anyway."

"And the stuff?" Terry asked.

"I'm backed up to your garage door." He raced through the kitchen, like I kid rushing to the tree on Christmas morning.

Carolyn followed us into the garage as Terry raised his garage door and we offloaded most of the backpacking items we had purchased earlier into the garage.

"Get anything you want to take with you out now," I told Carolyn.

"What? We not going backpacking? Not going into the woods?" I thought..."

"I know you thought, and let's hope anyone following us will think the same thing. I never said we were going hiking," I said. She seemed disappointed and ruffled through the bags until she pulled out the clothes she had bought and a couple of the high-intensity flashlights.

Terry shook my hand, "I can't believe you're doing this, man, this is some sick gear."

"Nah, I owe you this time," I said. I thanked him and gave him a quick hug. "Stay safe," he told me.

"Remember, keep this stuff out of sight. Don't give it away; don't sell it, for at least 60 days, OK? Do not stand out."

"Sure thing, Mr. Max."

***

We went back to the two vehicles, with all of our baggage now in the rental Expedition. Carolyn followed me to the Byron Herbert Reece memorial next to the Neels Gap Visitors Center on US 129, where the Appalachian Trail crosses between Blairsville and Cleveland, Georgia. She parked, and I told her to lock it, leave it, and get in with me.

"What's that all about?" she said.

"Distraction," I answered. "Anyone looking for us will follow your credit cards to the outdoor stores. They will see the backpacking purchases and maybe even our faces if they check the store surveillance video if they can access it. It is hard to know how deep the cartel tentacles go. Hopefully, they will put two and two together and start looking for us in backpacking areas.

"They will eventually find my SUV here, where many people park when hiking the trail. They will have to check out the trail; although if it were me, I'd send a team from Neel's Gap north and start another team down from North Carolina, starting from the Nantahala. If we did leave from here on foot, they could find us in a few days. It's hard to move fast on foot."

"I'm beginning to be more impressed. Meanwhile, where will we be?"

"Ever been to Myrtle Beach?" I asked.

"No, but I always wanted to go there," she smiled back, the first real smile I had seen on her since we met.

Chapter 30

I drove into Huntington for one last bit of business before leaving the mountains for the coast. Hopefully, if someone was after us, they would start in the mountains looking for a mountain boy rather than on the flatland along the coast.

I went to Allen's for my paperwork in the name of JJ Madison. He took the eight grand cash I gave him, went to the new chain bank that had recently opened a branch in Huntington, and opened a joint account in the name of him and JJ Madison. He asked for a rush on the debit cards.

While he was gone and Carolyn played with Street in his office, tossing a rag doll Allen kept on top of his file cabinet just for Street's visits, I stepped unseen behind the building a few feet into the woods where, with a shovel from Allen's tool shed I dug a small hole and dropped an emergency stash of $3000, the half-dozen gold coins and a bag of used silver dollars. I carefully covered up the Pelican case and recovered the spot at the base of the oak with moss and leaves so that it looked undisturbed.

Allen returned with the paperwork and I watched as he burned his copies. There would be no paper trail left in his office.

I signed the signature card for the bank. It was supposed to be signed on premises but knowing everyone in a small town as Allen did has its advantage. "They said I will have the cards FedEx tomorrow," he said. "I'll send them to you as soon as I get an address."

"Great, and thanks, brother."

"Semper Fi," he grinned. "You need anything you call."

"I know. Stay light," I said.

I drove out of Huntington, my home, wondering when I would be able to return. Carolyn was not wistful, instead acting excited, as if we were on a great adventure. Her confidence in us covering our tracks was greater than mine. I knew we were fleeing on a prayer and hoping for some luck.

"What did he say to you when we left?" she asked.

"Semper Fi."

"Were you in the Army?"

"No, Marines. Force Recon."

"So you're like a badass or something," she asked, intrigue in her voice.

"No. A Marine should cover it."

"And Allen was a Marine too?"

"Yeah, same outfit," I said.

"He seemed nice. It was nice of him to do this for you."

"Brother."

"He's your brother?"

"No," I said. "We few, we happy few, we band of brothers, for any man that sheds his blood with me today shall be my brother."

"Damn, you are surprising, quoting Shakespeare," she said.

"Everyone knows parts of the St. Crispin's speech," I said.

"Not everyone," she said. "So, he has shed his blood with you?"

"Yes," I said, saying nothing more.

"Iraq?"

"No. Afghanistan."

"You've been wounded then?"

"Twice."

"Purple heart? Wow, I'm traveling with a hero," Carolyn said.

"More like someone who is unlucky," I said. "Wrong place, wrong time."

"And Allen?"

"He was with me. You might say we saved each other's lives."

"What happened?"

"I don't ever talk about it. I'm here, he's here. 'Nuff said." Carolyn paused,

"Have you ever killed anyone, Max?"

I glared at her without answering. I had already told her I didn't talk about it.

Chapter 31

It was supposed to be a nothing-special trip that day in Afghanistan. Major Donnelly wanted to meet with a tribal elder in this dust choking tiny mud-walled cluster of dirty buildings 20 klicks off base, intelligence thing that Sergeants like me are not told about. The call had been unexpected, and the Major needed to move quick.

Allen and I were in the mess hall, killing time before our next mission out of Camp Leatherneck. The LT comes in and says the Major needs a couple of volunteers and it looks like we are it. "Nothing better to do," I said.

Allen was pulled in to come along too, as was Schwartz, the new kid from New Jersey who had not been on a mission yet and was gung-ho eager. We loaded in a Humvee, carrying a couple of radios and grabbing some extra magazines. I've never regretted carrying too much ammo.

Schwartz had a SAW, and off we went into the Helmed nether lands for what I learned later was supposed to be arranging a payoff to some tribal elder.

What we didn't know was that the Taliban had gotten wind of it, got there first and wired the hut with an IED. The Major had taken a liking to Schwarz and asked him to go inside with him and the elder as Allen and I stood guard outside.

Schwarz handed Allen the SAW, took Allen's M4, and about 10 seconds after they were inside the thing blew.

It knocked us down, perforated the grill of the Humvee, and leveled the hut into a pile of rubble. Had the blast not knocked us down we would have been cut down by the fusillade of bullets that followed from the well-planned ambush.

Allen had a hole in his lower thigh, I had a tear in my left bicep, and that was when the Taliban came in to mop up. It took both of us hobbling together to get into the rubble of the hut, where a little of the remaining wall gave us some cover.

I used to quote Kipling around the camp, especially things from "Barrack Room Ballads," written when he was accompanying Brit troops in Afghanistan in the 1870's. The one refrain that kept running through my mind, as we were forting up in the rubble:

"When you're wounded and left on Afghanistan's plains,

And the women come out to cut up your remains,
Just roll to your rifle and blow out your brains
And go to your God like a soldier."

The SAW was functional, and for the next 20 minutes we had an Old West shootout that I hoped and prayed didn't end like the Alamo. "The last belt," I heard Allen say before the last rush. I had already loaded my last magazine.

Luck arrived in the form of a road clearance unit with a belt-fed 40mm grenade launcher on top of a Buffalo, and they roared right into the middle of things just like the old US Cavalry in a Western.

Once there they began spreading death and mayhem, kicking ass, taking names, tearing up things and killing people, as good Marines are supposed to do.

Along the way, they rescued two shot up Marines and recovered what was left of two American bodies.

I had a round through my calf too by then, a hole through my shoulder just under my collarbone that barely missed an artery, and Allen would lose his leg below the knee. I passed out as the medics got to me, so I do not recall many of the specifics after the relief came.

My friends that visited us in the hospital afterward said I had half a magazine left and Allen was dry in the SAW, holding his Beretta and on his last magazine for it when they arrived. They counted nine dead Taliban close to us, but Allen had the majority of those with the SAW. I knew I got two coming in from my side for sure. One was close enough that I could see he was an old man who had no damn business doing what he was doing—but he paid for that mistake. He was close enough that some of his blood splattered on me. That was too close. The second was a teenage kid with an AK following right behind.

Our wounds were bad enough for a discharge and the LT put us in for medals, but nothing came of it. I was happy enough with a good paper discharge and the Purple Heart—and my ticket home. Allen followed a few months in the hospital and opened his car lot.

If there were medals to be given, they should have gone to the Major and Schwartz—they gave all they had to give, or at the very least those road clearance boys who did not hesitate to roll right into the middle of an already full-fledged firefight. Allen felt the same. Together we tried to readjust to civilian life.

"I can hobble around on one leg and sell cars with no trouble," he'd say during the nights we would split a bottle of single malt, smoke good cigars, and talk of the old days—not the good old days, just the old days.

I never talked to civilians about it—they would never understand. It was not too long after I returned and back in my advertising job that things went South with Carolyn III. Allen was good at listening as my marriage crumbled around me.

Chapter 32

I had planned to be clear of Huntington in the early afternoon, but the sun was sinking late in the day by the time we left Allen's. I felt better with no one knowing exactly where we were headed, and when Carolyn mentioned she was tired I decided to stop a couple of hours out of Huntington and get an early start in the morning. I began to look for a hotel as soon as we hit the four-lane highway.

There was still enough light for Carolyn to keep looking across the seat and out my window at the river as we wound through the Nantahala Gorge.

"It's beautiful," she said.

"Yes. The name means "land of the noonday sun", that's about the only time direct sunlight hits because of the depth of the gorge and the height of the mountains."

As we started on the four-lane outside Bryson City Carolyn got back to asking about Allen. I think she took the hint that I didn't talk about Afghanistan.

"Your friend Allen," she said.

"Brother."

"OK, your brother Allen, he's not really your brother, right?"

"He's not my mother's son. You might say twin sons of different mothers." I said, quoting the title of an old Dan Fogelberg and Tim Weisberg album. I didn't think she would have a clue who that was.

"You have trusted him with everything that could get us caught."

"Yes, I trust him with my life." I glanced at her. That was not a satisfactory explanation.

"I met him in high school when the small feeder elementary schools' students joined the larger county high school. A group of the rednecks was giving him crap. It had become known he was half-Cherokee. They were taunting him, calling him "Chief", stuff like that—and he was taking none of it, called the biggest bully out, Earl Soneman, and they went to the end of the building where the rednecks and white trash hung. It didn't last long; Allen kicked his ass.

"The problem was two of Earl's redneck friends didn't like their bud getting whipped and were going to join in. I didn't like Earl anyway—so I said, 'Two on one is not going to work. I'll even it up if you want a fair fight." They cowered away, and Allen and I were friends since.

"It was a fluke we ended up in the same outfit in the Marines. I was in a few months ahead of him."

"OK, makes sense, I guess. If you trust him."

I laughed, "In the history class they called us Grant and Sherman, after Mr. Anderson read the quote from Sherman, "Grant stood by me when I was crazy, I stood by him when he was drunk, and now we stand by each other, always."

Carolyn gave me a puzzled look. I realized history was not her long suit. I started to explain but I saw the eye roll before I finished the first sentence.

We took two rooms in Asheville with a connecting door at the Hampton Inn. I stay there out of habit because I usually get the points when I charge to my credit card. I paid cash this time and did not mention my Hilton Honors membership. We opened the two connecting doors between the rooms and left them cracked.

I brought a small empty duffle and once I set her bags into her room, I tossed it on her bed.

"What's this?"

"A bug out bag," I said. "This is the one bag you grab when you do not have time to grab anything else. Keep one change of clothes, cap, jacket, all which you can use to change your look quickly. I have already put a baby Glock, the 27 .40 cal in the side pocket with three magazines. Do not worry that two extend beyond the grip, they hold more rounds and will fit."

I took a few minutes to run her through the specs on the Glock, dry firing it a couple of times on a plastic dummy round, added a fresh magazine and put one up the spout. "Now all you have to do is pull the trigger. When the slide locks open, hit the button and eject the empty magazine, put a loaded one in, pull back on the slide and you are good to go again."

Carolyn listened attentively but was not happy that I felt she should know all this.

"Why do I need to know this when I have that .38?"

"Because you may not be able to get to the .38. Pack the bag," I said. "I'm doing the same, you have the leather duffle, I'm taking the canvas."

"Why separate bags?"

"Because we may not always be able to go in the same direction." I caught the shiver that shook her entire body. "Don't worry, this is only a precaution. I like to be redundant. I'd have two motors in a car if I could, just in case one quit working."

Carolyn gave a soft laugh. "OK." I went into my room and packed my own bug out bag, putting in the Glock 22 and four magazines, jeans, cap, reversible workout tee, jacket, and a wicked sharp dagger handmade by Daniel

Winkler from Blowing Rock. The knife was an old reliable friend dating back to the Helmed.

The stress of the day and the adrenaline fading once we got horizontal knocked us both into a solid sleep that only ended with a beating on my door and an Oriental woman shouting "ousekeeping."

***

"Will this work? All these things we are doing to cover our trail?" Carolyn asked after we had crossed into South Carolina after she had spent over an hour of travel without speaking, lost in thought, staring out the window.

"For a while," I said. "It depends."

"Depends on what?"

"Ask me if we are still alive in two weeks."

Chapter 33

Two wrecks and construction made it a long slow drive to Myrtle Beach, and Carolyn was not talkative.

"I'm not much for a conversation on trips—and I've never been in this part of the world before, it is interesting. You drive. I'll sightsee," she said. I was content to listen to talk radio and drive.

We stopped at a Pilot Travel Center for gas; I filled the tank while she got sandwiches in the Subway. A liquor store was across the street. At her request I pulled in and we put in a stock of vodka and I lucked into a bottle of Weller 12-year-old bourbon. As we got back on the road, she was a bit more talkative—or inquisitive.

"Why do you have so many guns?" she asked.

"I like them. Always have. Grandad loved them, Dad loved them, like keeping on the family tradition. And I'm always looking for the perfect one. Each firearm I own has an attribute I like, but I am still looking for the one with all the attributes I like. I enjoy the search."

Carolyn looked back in the Expedition. "Bags too, huh?"

"Yeah, I am searching for the perfect bag too—still not found."

"And women?" That one stung.

"Evidently, if history is any proof. Enjoy the scenery," I said, ending the conversation as I turned the radio louder. She took the hint and turned back to the window.

It was after dark when we arrived in Myrtle Beach.

Some big event had filled every room in Myrtle, so I turned to North Myrtle Beach, pulling into a condo unit that had a neon sign reading "Vacancy". I asked for two bedrooms, and the young clerk with the dark framed glasses seemed annoyed that I had interrupted his reading. He explained he only had one room left.

"Two beds then," I said.

The clerk did not answer. He lay the book down, stood, and asked for my ID. I thought he looked a little too close at it, but he returned it with no question. "Actually it is a two-bedroom condo, so it is the same as two rooms, each with its own bath," he said.

"I did get a strange look when I told him I preferred to pay cash for the room. I paid three days in advance.

"Most people use credit cards," he said.

"Most people do not have a wife on the same credit card account that spends like my wife and keeps the damn thing maxed," I said, looking over at Carolyn. She glared back. "We stopped to buy gas and my card was declined. That was when she told me she had gone on a shopping spree for new clothes for the trip. I'd rather pay cash than suffer the further embarrassment of my card coming up declined."

"Tell me about it," the clerk said. "I have the same problem—with my wife."

I took the keys, hung the paper tag from the condo from the rearview and loaded the bags on to the cart. As we went back into the parking lot Carolyn looked up. "I maxed out your card? Asshole."

Chapter 34

There was a surprise when I opened the door. It was large, with a kitchen, oversized living room with sliding doors facing the ocean from the 5th floor, but only one bedroom. There was the couch. "You can take the ocean view," I said.

"Good, I like waking up looking at the ocean," Carolyn said. "It was what I liked best about Santa Barbara."

***

I scrutinized the room. Beach rental décor, wood fake bamboo frame chairs with seashell cushions, sea oats and ocean foam print that would be the same in every unit, a sliding glass door with sand and grit in the track, and as usual a too-loud noisy heat-air unit. Carolyn walked into the bedroom.

The couch appeared to be a hide-a-bed, and very uncomfortable. Perhaps I could pull the foam mattress and sleep on the floor.

Carolyn looked at me with a questioning stare when she came back into the room and saw me laying the phone back into its cradle. "I was talking to the desk. You want the good news or the bad news?" I said as I hung up the phone.

"Let me guess, this is a take it or leave it room."

"You got it. This is what they call a two-bedroom. Don't worry, I'll make do on the couch."

"Damn, aren't you all Mr. Prim and Proper," Carolyn gave a soft giggle. She gilled just giggled. I was stunned.

"You have another option?" I asked.

"If you can keep your hands to yourself you can sleep in the bed with me," she said. "Maybe you could get on top of the sheet and I will get under it, for my own protection."

"Not a bad idea actually," I said. "You may not know me as well as you think. You never know what urges might hit me in my sleep, like sleepwalking, you know."

"I'm learning, I am learning," Carolyn said. "Let me unpack, why don't you pour us a drink and we can sit on the balcony and look out at the ocean and unwind."

I poured two Vodka martinis and took mine to the balcony, taking a chair. The table was shoved into the balcony corner, and there was a chaise lounge beside the chair.

Carolyn joined me and had changed into a long white tee that fell almost to her knees. It was thin, and the night air made an enticing view. She had removed her makeup and her hair was down. She was beautiful. At another time with different threats, the way the moon was pouring light from the reflection on the water, the steady crash of the surf on the beach; in different circumstances, it might have even been romantic, I thought.

We had the first drink without speaking and I refilled the glasses. Carolyn spoke without turning away from the ocean.

"I'm scared, Max."

"Should be," I said. "There are nine or ten ways this can end, eleven of them are bad."

"Can we do this? Can you protect me?" She looked at me with moist doe eyes almost to the point of tears. Her eyes sought reassurance, looked for hope.

"I think so," I lied. I knew we couldn't run forever, and with a cartel on our trail, it was not likely to end well. I remember watching the takedown of Carolyn's home and the two cops murdered. Those guys knew what they were doing—and were probably hot behind us. I didn't know which cartel. I knew the Zetas had a lot of former Mexican Special Forces in their ranks. Whoever it was, it did not bode well for us.

I didn't lie when I told her, "I'm willing to die trying to protect you." She didn't break her gaze from my eyes.

"Yes, I think you mean that." She took her hand from the arm of the chaise lounge and laid it on top of mine. Her hand was warm and soft. "Do you hate me? For getting you into this? I had no idea it would go like this, really. I'm sorry."

"I think I got myself into this," I said.

We had finished our second drinks. "My turn," Carolyn volunteered, rising from the chaise lounge and clanking around in the kitchen before emerging with a drink in each hand. She reached over me and set mine down on the table, careful not to splash the liquid in the shallow martini glass. She sat hers down beside it but instead of retaking her seat she straddled my lap, taking my face between her two hands, staring into my eyes she said, "You make me feel safe, Max." Then she kissed me.

Oh my God, she kissed me. A shock of current ran from my lips through my body to my toes. Through her lips, she locked on to my soul and held on tight.

It was at that moment for the first time she let down her facade and I saw the real woman she was, no pretense, no arrogance, no wall. A dream, it had to be a dream. A dream from which I dared not wake up, a dream I prayed was not a dream.

I responded as well, stroking, touching, caressing, no conscious move, but flowing, reacting to her reaction, to her touch. There was no step-by-step kiss, grope breast, lift top, kiss breast 1-2-3 progression, there was no thought, only flow, each touch, each step more forward than the previous one, so natural, like it was meant to happen in this order, a river of emotion filled with rapids and eddies. There was no thinking, my mind on overload begging to absorb the softness, the movement of her muscles flexing under the flesh, the hot touch of her, the sounds of her breathing, her taste.

We floated into the bedroom. There was no urgent tearing off our clothes, it was like a soft wind drifted through the door, pushed her long tee over her head, and lifted us weightless and deposited us on the bed.

Then it was two intertwined bodies, flesh against hot flesh, hardness, softness, fingertip caresses and kissing everywhere, our mouths melding together. It was a kaleidoscope of sensations, a dreamy billowing blur of colors that even now comes back to me in split-second glimpses of that moment. It was looking in her eyes, watching them widen as our bodies joined, the smile of the pleasure, the gasps, the thin line of sweat on her upper lip that I licked away, the clutching hands on my ass and the final yielding of tensed muscles losing control and the collapsing weakness that followed.

We clung together until we could no longer, and then lay to our backs, our bodies cooling in the slow current from the ceiling fan. I traced the outline of the rose tattoo on her shoulder with a fingertip.

"Wow. That was nice, Max. Really nice." She noticed my touch. "I got the tat in college."

"It looks good on you."

"Roses are supposed to stand for love," Carolyn said. "When I had it done, I was convinced there was still such a thing in this world. Now I'm not so sure."

I didn't rise to the bait of that statement and brought the subject back to our lovemaking. "I'm glad you think it was nice, Mrs. Madison. Impressive. I'm not sure I can stand right now, my knees are weak." I said.

"Maybe this playing house is not so bad," she said.

"Or maybe it is," I said.

"What do you mean?"

"We cannot let emotion cause us to lose our focus," I said.

"Who said anything about emotion," Carolyn said. "We had a good fuck." I felt the wall coming back up. Her protective metal shell back in place as the magic moment faded away. "Keep your damn focus," she spat. She turned to her side away from me, pulling the covers up to her shoulder.

Chapter 35

I was up two hours before her, on my third coffee when she stepped into the living room with puffy eyes and mussed hair. Oh hell, I thought to myself, she is beautiful even first thing in the morning.

They say that men are seduced by their eyes, women by their ears, but I am only qualified to speak about the male point of view. I subscribe to the theory, but with a woman like Carolyn, there is also the understanding that a woman that looks like that has every man fall in love with her a little, based only on appearance. Maybe it is the trophy aspect, but more likely it is the simple allure of a beautiful woman.

They say that babies react more positively to pretty women than plain women. Most men never grow out of that. I guess I am typical.

Carolyn poured her coffee, tasted it, grimaced, and put it in the microwave, reheating it. Once it chimed, she came into the living room, taking a seat in the easy chair. She said nothing of the night before. "OK, what's the plan?"

"I've been busy," I said. "Nothing unusual at home, Daniel in LA says he may have a prospect, and I have two names, one in Seattle, one in Virginia near DC. I will call them and feel them out.

"I see disposing of the sword as our only option. Once the sword is out of our hands and your brother and his friends see there is no connection or damage to him, your brother and his venture with the Japanese will follow its own course. Not our concern. If the sword can be tied back to him, it endangers the deal. So, we have to get it to new owners without ever having your name attached."

"Tricky."

"Yes."

"About last night," she said finally.

"What about it?"

"I do not fall in love with everyone I fuck. It is a physical need, not emotional. You shouldn't expect anything more than what it was. It was fun. Do not read anything into it. Keeping your focus keeps me safe. I won't let having sex with you be a distraction."

"You are distracting in a cute sort of way."

"You think having sex will cause you to lose your focus? If that is the case, then there will be no more sex. I see sex only as recreation anymore. I've tried the emotional and love side of it—it's not worth the trouble and pain that comes with it."

"Fine," I said. "I hate to say it, but I agree with you. The love and the pain were not worth it—most of the time." She looked at me with her head tilted. "Nah, I'm lying, there were times when I was in love, it was worth the pain," I said.

"Oh hell, one of those," she said, "I knew it."

"What?"

"A white knight. One of those romantic good guys on the white horse."

"I don't have a white horse, I only have Street," I said.

"I'm surprised you don't have a horse. Your SUV is white though."

"You got me there." I was relieved when she changed the subject.

"Now what about your leads? Do you have a customer yet?"

"We wait until I hear more; I have put out the feelers. We hang around here long enough to get the debit cards Allen is sending." I said.

"I'm going to the Kroger for some groceries and a few things," she said.

"I'll go with you," I said.

"No. I need to get away from you for a while," she said. "You need to clear your head."

"Wait," I said, "Be sure you have the .38. Keep your hand on it inside the purse while walking to the store and as soon as you exit the store, understand?"

"Yes, I do."

"And remember what I said; if you pull it don't try to scare someone. When you pull it, you pull the trigger. No hesitation. Your life depends on it."

"I get it," she said.

"Have you ever heard of the 3-3-3 rule?"

"No."

"It is based on a rough interpretation of FBI statistics. The average gunfight is at three feet, with three rounds fired, and lasts three seconds."

"Three seconds?"

"Yes. So, the first person that fires is going to be the winner. Keep your hand on the pistol when you leave the building."

"I understand."

"How about I drive you and wait in the parking lot?" I asked. She did not answer, only took the keys off the counter walked out the door.

***

I assume we talked after she returned, but I do not remember about what. She had stopped at the liquor store and brought all the liquors for Long Island Tea, going top shelf: Gray Goose Vodka, Contreau, Beefeaters Gin, Patron tequila, and Old Guadalupe Caribbean rum.

"My treat," she said. "We're due for a good drunk, take the edge off. We drink now and have brunch."

I started to protest but relented. This might be the last time I dared for a while. I knew we had a small lead on the possible pursuit, with friends as a buffer and no one except Allen knowing where we were. "Sounds like a plan," I said, as she mixed the drinks.

We both knew where it would end up—and having mutually declared it was not for emotion, only release, by the second drink with a light buzz I asked her to take her top off. "I'm a boob man, and you have exceptional ones," I said. "Forgive me if I want to look at them."

Carolyn stood and crossed her arms, pulling her top over her head, and at the same time unbuttoned her jeans and removed them. She was going commando. "Nudity doesn't both me," she said as if trying to shock me, going one step beyond my request. "My late husband and I went to Orient Beach on St. Martin for vacation a couple of times. We didn't put on clothes for days. It felt really weird when we put on clothes for the trip home." She giggled, "There they call people that wear clothes 'textiles'. I think the world might be a lot more interesting if no one ever wore clothes."

"With a body like yours it would certainly separate you from everyone else," I said. She only smiled in return, as if I was reaffirming what she already knew.

I sipped my drink and enjoyed the view, the soft swaying of her bare breasts, a symphony of their movement as she shifted position on the couch. Her beauty may not have been perfect enough for Hollywood, but she was the most beautiful woman with whom I had ever shared any intimacy. And there was something other than her beauty that appealed to me, though I couldn't put my finger on it.

Despite all the misgivings and what I said, I felt emotion creeping in around the edges. Was she the one Carolyn that would be the right one, or yet another in a long line of different firearms, bags, and women who looked great at the start, but the flaws soon began to appear?

I pushed the thought out of my mind by the third drink and we were kissing on the couch. I went floating back into the bedroom with the fair Carolyn for a second romp. We stopped only for sandwiches and more drinking then back to bed. If it was only physical, then enjoy the physical. Sometime along the way, I passed out and awoke in the morning to the smell of ham cooking.

Chapter 36

Carolyn scrambled ham and eggs with a splash of Tabasco sauce and sprinkled with Mexican cheese. It was delicious. We were both hungry and finished quickly.

I made more calls while she cleaned up the kitchen and puttered about. Eventually, she sat back down with a fresh cup of coffee.

"And I learn you cook, too?" I said, "I'm surprised."

"I was raised in Arizona. Grandad had a ranch. Everyone pitched in to do whatever was needed to be done. Cooking was a part of it. As I said, there's a lot about me you don't know."

"I want to. Tell me more."

"That's some of the good parts of my life," she said. "Mom was a free spirit and had this thing for musicians. I guess you could say she was a groupie, and after years away, she showed back up at Grandad and Grandma's with Thomas, who was the seven-year-old grandson they had never laid eyes on before.

"Mom must have gotten restless. After a year and a half, she left Thomas with Grandma and disappeared again—until she showed back up on their doorstep years later pregnant with me. She told me later that she wasn't certain who my father was, that I was conceived in what she said was a large party that involved what she called, "several possibilities". I took my grandparents' surname.

"We lived in a trailer next to Grandad and Grandma. Thomas and I were raised there. Mom always made poor choices in men and would disappear for weeks at a time, until I was sixteen when she disappeared and never came home. They found her dead in Phoenix later that year. Overdose."

I nodded as she continued, paying attention to the movement of her full lips as much as I was paying attention to what she said.

"Thomas is nine years older than me, so it is not like we were close. When he was 16, I was seven, and that was when he started getting in trouble. He always ran with trash and it pulled him down.

"Grandad finally sent him off to a military school for his Junior and Senior years, he said that would put some straightness in his backbone, but it didn't. I moved in with Grandad and Grandma then, at their insistence. I thought I was a big girl and could live alone, but you didn't argue with Grandad.

"Thomas squeaked through college and managed to get a job at the battery manufacturer. He rose through the ranks quickly."

"So, he has some smarts in addition to being paranoid and crazy?"

Carolyn looked at me with no expression. "Not at all. You want to know how he rose through the ranks so quickly? He spent a year in an entry-level management position.

"Then his boss changes jobs—moves to Kentucky because someone had threatened his teenage daughter. The company is famed for elevating people up from within. Thomas was willing to take advantage of rising through the ranks, but he would help it along.

"Thomas had some of his druggie friends grab the man's daughter one night and scare her. It was enough for the boss. He left town; Thomas got that job.

"His next supervisor was discovered with half a kilo of coke in his car, although he tested negative for drug use and had a line of character witnesses a mile long. The supervisor claimed someone had planted the drugs, but it didn't matter. he's gone, Thomas moves up. I think Thomas had the drugs planted."

"I don't like the way this is going," I said.

"Neither did his supervisors," Carolyn said. "Thomas was third down from the top by then and working deals with some drug smugglers from Mexico. That supervisor had a bad car wreck, was T-boned by a dump truck driven by a drunk illegal who vanished from the scene of the accident before the cops got there. The driver was never found.

"The vice-president of the company was murdered in a robbery; you know how it is in those border towns. By this time the President of the company saw the writing on the wall and took early retirement, but he kept a seat on the board at Thomas' request, to help rubber stamp everything Thomas wanted to be done."

"But they still managed to come up with the battery technology, right?" I asked.

"Thomas had help from his Mexican friends on all this. We inherited some warehouses on the border, and it was his idea to start a tunnel from the American side. He bought my share of the inheritance early on and he thought I didn't know what was happening."

"How did you find out?"

"Rumors, an old boyfriend who nearly shit his pants when he found out Thomas McMasters was my big brother. My boyfriend was into weed, selling enough that he could clear what he used himself and he knew a lot about my brother. It ended my romance because the boyfriend was so afraid of Thomas. He was a cute guy too," Carolyn said.

"As for the patents and the battery technology, Thomas had heard of the inventor with the patents. The inventor approached the company, and the early tests proved that the inventor had something, that it could work.

Thomas couldn't let it go at that. He wanted it all. His Mexican friends paid the inventor a visit, and that night the patents were purchased at a very agreeable cash price with no royalties. A few months later the inventor died in a home invasion robbery where he lived up in Indiana. Convenient, huh?"

"You're not making this up, are you?"

"I wish I was," Carolyn said. "With that as background, I know that Thomas will not want to leave anyone alive that has any knowledge of the sword. Leopards do not change their spots."

I stared out at the ocean, her story reaffirming the pile of shit we were in and made it several turds deeper.

We laid down for a quick nap that lasted longer than I expected. When I awoke and was washing my face, I heard from the living room, "I'm hungry, Mr. Madison. Take your wife to lunch," she giggled.

***

After we returned from lunch at the Flying Fish, enjoying the smoked mahi-mahi while overlooking the intercostal waterway, we returned to the condo and took a walk down the beach toward the Cherry Grove pier. We rented bicycles and rode further down. I had a flashback of riding bicycles with a girl named Carolyn, right down to feeling the pain and angst of those days. It helped reinstate what I call my Carolyn caution.

We turned in the bicycles and began to walk back. As we walked, she took my hand and we stepped together hand in hand down the beach. "I've always wanted to walk hand in hand down the beach with a lover," she said, "Haven't you?"

"You mean you've never done this before?" I asked. Having lived in view of a beach only a fool would not take a woman like Carolyn on a walk down the beach—if nothing more as an excuse to see her in a bikini.

Carolyn may have been in a daydream when she made that remark, or simply trying to play me as she could play most men, but she didn't like being challenged. She jerked her hand away and moved away from me, walking faster. I let her go.

Chapter 37

Back in the condo I had a call on my phone. The call evolved longer than I had expected. I glanced into the bedroom. Carolyn was fast asleep on the bed with the comforter pulled half around her. I closed the door quietly. She was up at three, I heard the shower running, and I stared as she walked naked from the bedroom to the fridge to retrieve a soda. She made no effort to cover herself and strode through the room as natural as if she was fully clothed. My expression must have said something else.

Carolyn stopped soda in hand, her magnificent nude body on full display. "It's not like you've not seen me naked already," she said. "Clothes have never been a major thing with me." She turned and disappeared back into the bedroom. "I'm not done with my nap," she said.

"I love your outfit," I yelled after her. When I went to the door she was already under the cover and her eyes closed. She was up in time for supper at Benny Rappas.

"Damn, you have good taste in restaurants," she said.

"I learned a long time ago that when you are on the road a decent restaurant is one of life's true pleasures," I said.

That night was not the passion filled sex of the previous two. "I'm not feeling up for anything," she said. "Could you just hold me?" She snuggled into my embrace, spooning. My hand fell to her breast.

"I don't have anywhere else to put my hand," I said, making it an excuse.

"Fine," she said.

I held that position long after she was in the rhythmic breathing of sleep. It had been a long time since I enjoyed drifting into sleep cuddling a woman—and waking up still beside her the next morning. This is nice, I thought, maybe too nice.

Chapter 38

I was on the phone again before she was up. I had received a lead from Daniel in LA and talked to his contact in Seattle. I tiptoed around the subject feeling him out and he quickly decided he wasn't interested.

I opened my laptop and opened a map of the Arizona border country. I located the small town she had mentioned, south of Antelope Falls. As I zoomed out my eyes hit Del Rio, and I thought of Briscoe Reddix. He was a potential buyer I had not considered. He liked guns, knives, swords, history, and moved freely back and forth across the border, even having a place near Lake Amistad.

I knew Briscoe had the cash if it was something he liked, being in the oil business, and I knew he had paid over $200,000 for a knife attributed to Jim Bowie's brother Rezin, because I had sold it to him--for cash without filling out the government paperwork. And even more important, I trusted him. When Carolyn finally got up, I only told her I had a new lead, adding few details.

I did not tell her who. No one would know where I was heading, not even Briscoe. I would call him from the road to set up a meet. It would be a two or three-day road trip with Carolyn. I looked forward to more sex, but that did not mean I was letting down that guard around my heart and forgetting about my Carolyn factor.

Just because we had fucked did not mean I should give her total trust. Enough women named Carolyn had taught me that in the past.

Chapter 39

"And the afternoon plans are?"

"Nothing planned," I said. "TV, movie, something like that? Or we can start drinking now."

"I do not watch much TV, how about a movie?"

"It's a date," I said.

"I've not been on a date in a long time. Do I get popcorn too?"

"And a drink if you wish."

"I wish." We drove to the multiplex at the mall and took the best of a meager offering of movies.

It was not much of a movie, a James Bond wannabe holding a snub-nose .38 taking on a platoon of bad guys with automatic weapons and full riot gear and emerging without a scratch. There were a lot of gasoline explosions, two nude scenes of bare-breasted women, and a weak love theme in which the heroine is killed in the end. As she was dying Carolyn pulled me over and whispered in my ear, "I hope that's not us."

"Don't worry," I said. "I don't carry a .38."

"But I do," she whispered back.

The ending did bother her though. She was silent on the drive back to the condo. Once inside she said, "I need a drink." She started again on the vodka martinis.

"Make me one too if you don't mind."

It was hot outside and the curtains were half drawn. We didn't turn on the light as we sat there quiet. "It was a shit movie," she finally said. "But that director always does crap."

"You sound like you are familiar with his work."

"I dated the asshole," she said, emptying her martini and refilling it, bringing me another as well. Then she walked back to the bar and made another, setting it down beside her first. "In Hollywood, once an asshole always an asshole, the only difference is if you are successful you are an asshole with money. The place uses you. You use too, or you get used."

"There are assholes everywhere," I said.

"Not per capita," Carolyn said. A strange look came over her face. "OK, you plied me with a movie, popcorn, and a soda. Take me to dinner and you might get lucky."

"I've always been lucky," I said. "Let's go."

We opted for a New York style pizza place in a strip mall and were back at the condo in bed by 8:30. We didn't start trying to sleep until 10.

Just before she dozed off, she sleepily said, "We're sleeping together, you've taken me on a date, to a movie, we've walked down a beach, and I'm carrying an ID that says I'm your wife."

"Yes."

"You need to be careful. People might think we're serious." In my own mind, there was a cynical thought-- a faint hope that she was there was a hint of serious behind her quip. I'd heard similar things from women named Carolyn before. I still did not have this Carolyn figured out—but I was content how things were going until I did.

Chapter 40

I left Carolyn sleeping in the bed, the covers back, nude, pausing at the door to admire her naked perfection, like a Botticelli Venus, reveling in the fact I had the privilege and opportunity to enjoy the pleasures of such a woman. No, it wasn't love. Not yet. But it was not merely the physical recreational sex that she called it, there was something more.

Downstairs the FedEx driver delivered a package with my debit cards from Allen, along with a note from him. "Couple of hard looking Hispanic guys are in town, looking around. Not saying much, just looking for the moment."

I took a coffee from the lobby pot, bought a local paper, and went back upstairs. Maybe our trail was not as cold as I had hoped, and as I replayed my careful steps. Where was a weak link that could bite us in the ass? I kicked myself for being so stupid. Terry. Terry was just a kid, and many people around town knew he worked for me part-time.

Anyone pursuing us would get around to him eventually. If they saw the backpacking gear it would add up quickly that he might be a conduit to us—and provide the evidence we were not on a hiking trail, eliminating my hoped-for wild goose chase diversion for our pursuers.

No one knew we were going to Myrtle Beach except Allen, and he was the one person in the world I knew would not talk. Terry was something else. He was young.

Would he tell them he made fake ID's for us; would he remember the names he assigned? Did he still have the files he had used to make the ID's on his computer? One way to find out. I dialed his number.

"Hello."

"Hey Terry, this is Max. Anyone been asking about me?"

"Well yeah, now that you mention it, he said he was an old Army buddy. Came by this morning."

"What did you say?"

"Nothing," Terry said. "I know you were a Marine, not the Army."

"Did he buy it?"

"I said you had told me you would not need me to come in to work for a couple of weeks, you were going out of town was all I knew. I said you had asked me to pick up the mail on Fridays and put any packages left outside in the storage building that I had the key to. He wanted to see the mail, but I told him I had not checked it yet, it was all still there. He left quickly after that. He didn't hang around."

"Terry, listen to me very closely, this is important. Keep that backpack stuff out of sight."

"It is, I put it in the attic actually. Mom couldn't pull her car in the garage."

"OK and destroy your computer. Now."

"Aw, come on Mr. Max, not my computer."

"I'll buy you a new one, the fastest biggest one known, one that when you turn it on the lights in the neighborhood will dim," I said.

"When? You know I cannot do without my computer. And I have to copy my files."

"That's what I'm worried about, the ID's you made. Do you remember the names you gave us?"

"No, I had a random generator pull them up, and I erased the files as soon as you left," Terry said.

"Could they be recovered from the hard drive?"

"Of course."

"Destroy the hard-drive then, I have to be sure those ID's can't be found."

"OK."

"Terry."

"Yes."

"Do it while I wait. This is a matter of life and death."

"Oh, all right," he said reluctantly. "Hang on, let me plug in my back up for my other stuff."

"Do you back up to the cloud?"

"Nah, I don't trust that stuff. Too easy to hack," he said. "OK, I'm moving my other files." I waited 10 minutes—on the phone.

"OK, that's got it. Hang on, let me take the back off." I could hear a clank or two. A grunt. Then Terry's voice again. "I'm at the grill on the back porch." I heard a whump. "I'm smashing it with a hammer. It is breaking it up pretty good. OK, now I'm pouring a charcoal lighter on it. Listen Mr. Max." I could hear the match striking and the WHOOSH of the flame catching.

"Damn," Terry said. "I must have put too much. I've singed the hair on my arm."

"You OK?"

"Yeah."

"The hard drive?"

"Terminal. God and all his angels couldn't get that thing going again. Hang on, someone's at the door." He had not hung up from the call. "Hey," I heard Terry say, "I thought I told you I didn't know where he was." I heard the whump of a fist hitting flesh and someone speaking Spanish. I hung up the phone and called Calvin, telling him to get a car over to Terry's fast, but go geared up.

I looked down at my phone. Fuck. Time for a new burner. They could trace this one to Myrtle Beach.

Carolyn was on the balcony having coffee, back in her flannel nightgown. "Trouble, we gotta go," I said. "We may be burned."

To her credit she didn't argue, hastily dressing in shorts and a blue button up blouse, throwing her clothes in the bags without folding them while I went downstairs for the cart. We were loaded within 10 minutes.

I laid the keys on the counter.

"Everything OK Mr. Madison? We have had cancellations, you stay can another day," the clerk said. He was the same clerk from the night we checked in.

"Look," I said, leaning over and motioning him to come closer. "I have something of a sticky situation here and need some help."

"Yes sir?" he said.

"That woman I've been with is not my wife. In fact, she is another man's wife, and she is divorcing him because of spousal abuse. He's almost killed her twice. He's very violent." The desk clerk nodded. "He was served with divorce papers while we were here; I wanted to get her out of town for her own safety. I'm sure he is going to send some guys looking for her. He's a building contractor out of Spartanburg and employees a lot of Mexicans, so the people looking for her will probably be Latino. I need some discretion here, understand?" I slid five $100 bills on the counter too him.

"I understand very clearly sir," he smiled. "Anything you need."

"They will probably have pictures of us and ask if you've seen us. We came in and you were full."

"Yes. That will work."

"Wipe away any record of our stay, and maybe the video recorder is acting up? So, there are no images of us?" He looked over his shoulder and back down at the five bills.

"Already done sir. I hope you enjoyed your stay."

"Indeed, I did," I said. "And if there are no repercussions when I return there will be five more of those for you. Are we clear?"

"Crystal clear, sir. Crystal clear. Thank you for staying with us." I watched as he went into the office and reset the video recorder. He thumbed through the registration cards, ripped them in front of me, and dropped them into the paper shredder. I gave him a thumbs up.

***

Carolyn was standing at the condo entrance watching. "What was that all about?"

"Trying to erase any record of our staying here," I said. "We're fleeing your abusive husband who was just served your divorce papers."

"Ohh I love it. Damn, I think I saw that movie. Julia Roberts wasn't it?"

"You're the movie star on this team."

"Oh, only if that were true," she smiled.

Chapter 41

We waited until we arrived in Florence to find another discount store for a burner. Carolyn had copied my contact numbers to a small notebook as I drove. I made some last calls on the old phone. First to Calvin. "Damn Max, what the fuck are you into, you have stirred up a hornet's nest."

"How's Terry?" I asked.

"A few lumps and bruises. Those guys were not happy finding the burned hard drive and thumped on him pretty good. Still thumping when Compton and Davis pulled up on them, locked and loaded like you said. Both bad guys were armed. Both with Arizona concealed carry licenses. They rented the old Gothe place on the lake through Blue Lake Realty; bill was paid for by some Desert Investigations out of Tempe, Arizona. You know anything about that?"

"No," I said.

"I told Terry to take the rest of his Spring Break in Daytona or somewhere, and his folks thought that was a good idea. He's on his way there now, although, with his face bruised up like that, I don't think he stands much of a chance of picking up any sweet young thing."

"As if the poor boy ever did," I laughed. "Charges on the bad guys?"

"Assault and battery. Carrying a gun in commission, they will bail out by Monday. Seems the judge is conveniently fishing somewhere out of cell range like I suggested to him, and of course, the court is closed on Sunday. That will give me time to see if I can think of anything else with which to charge them. Somebody kicked in the door of your office, by the way, riffled through things pretty good. We couldn't find any prints, but we know who did from what Terry said. I'll tie them into it before it's over—but they will be on the street on bail either way."

"I have security cameras in the office, get a pen and I'll give you the login and password so you can download the footage."

"That should do it. Shoot," Calvin said. I gave him the info.

"Thanks for taking care of Terry."

"It's my fucking county," Calvin said. "Outsiders coming in here and thinking they can do shit in my county. Anyone thinking that has got another think coming, and that thing coming is one pissed off sheriff in the form of me." He snickered.

"That's not all," he said. "Those two guys were not alone. Old ugly Mexican looking fellow and a taller one with a hook nose stopped by Allen's asking about you, said they were your old Army buddy. You believe that, saying that to Allen?

"Well cool as day he says sure, he has all your contact info, just to wait right there—and he comes out with an AR and the laser sight on one's head. Made them lay face down there in the car lot. Takes both their guns, both carrying those new FN 5.7's, and Allen told them he would introduce them to you by sending them to hell right then if they wanted to go, and they can wait there for the introduction because he figures you and he will get there soon enough.

"They had the good sense to leave without their weapons. I tried to catch them before they left the county, but they were over the state line and into Georgia and gone before I knew it."

"Think they will be back?" I asked.

"I sure as hell hope so, it's been a long time since I really fucked someone up for resisting arrest, but I think those two top my list. Seems them boys we caught out at Terry's ran into resisting arrest problems from my deputies. Beating on a kid they had it coming."

"Glad things are OK there."

"Good enough," Calvin said, adding, "Max, I don't know what kind of shit you are in, but you know there is not a lot I can do outside Oconoluftee County."

"I know. I don't expect you to. Thanks for what you've done Calvin."

"You get home I can take better care of you boy," he said.

"Thanks. I'll see you soon."

***

I hung up and dialed Allen. "Heard you had a problem or two?"

"Nothing I can't handle," he said. "Army. dumb motherfuckers. I should have shot them for that alone. Thinking you were not a Marine."

"You may still get your chance. You feel like doing some traveling if I need it?"

"Where and when is all I need to know," he said. "I can get Connie to handle the car lot and feed your mangy old mutt for a few days."

I laughed. Connie and Allen thought as much of Street as I did. Connie had asked me to will the dog to her in case anything ever happened to me. "No need to will him to you," I told her. "Street will come here automatically if I'm not around; he's been here so much."

I told Allen, "I'll get back with you, but keep a travel bag packed," I said. "I might need you on short notice."

"Copy that," he said.

I went into the big box store in Florence and bought a new burner phone. As I walked by a ¾ ton Ford pickup with a long canvas covered trailer, New York plates, I slid the old phone up under the tarp until I heard it fall with a clunk into the bed.

We stopped at a small grocery store for a bathroom break, not a chain store and less likely to have surveillance cameras. I backed into the space to the side with nothing but trees behind me and raised the back as if I were getting something from our luggage. I was. Four screws out and four screws back in and I had a new tag number for the Expedition in the form of Allen's second dealer plate.

If I was acting paranoid it was because I was. Things were unwinding much faster than I anticipated, which meant anyone chasing us would likely be closer than I thought. It was not a time to make a misstep.

Chapter 42

Carolyn didn't ask where we were going until I was heading south on I-95. "Now what?" she said.

"Did you like Texas?"

"There were some things I did like about Texas," she said.

"Sooner or later you are going to have to tell me where you have that sword hidden," I said.

"Well if we are going to Texas, you're getting warmer, how's that."

"Close enough for the moment I guess," I said.

"Good. It will have to be."

"Don't trust me yet?" I asked.

"No, it is more like I don't trust myself. I don't want to panic and start thinking that giving this sword to my brother is going to fix anything."

***

My next call was to Briscoe Reddix. "Hey there Max, you getting' any pussy," he laughed with his usual greeting.

"All I can stand," I said.

"That's my boy. What is up with you? Found me something nice?"

"Maybe. Want to talk to you about it face to face if that's all right. You gonna be around a few days? I'm coming through your way."

"Hell yeah, be glad to have ya," he said. "I'll get the guest cottage air turned on."

"See you then."

***

Carolyn was content looking at the window, but there are only so many pine thickets one can see before they all start running together and eventually, she wanted conversation. We were in Georgia before that began.

I learned more about my traveling companion as we rode. She likes to nap—a lot. She doesn't like to talk, preferring to listen to the radio or Pandora.

When I first turned the radio on it was on some modern country station. She changed it. "I hate that shit, that's not country," she said. "Garth Brooks, Alan Jackson, Blackhawk, Restless Heart, that's country, that and 60's rock. It is what was played in my house growing up. I still like it."

"No Hip-hop?"

"I was raised on a ranch remember. No hip-hop." She found a late 60's early 70's link on Pandora, plugged it in through the line-in cord and her phone.

"That what you like?" I asked.

"Yeah."

"Me too, but I like a little of everything."

"Such as?"

"Dave Koz, Bob James."

"Soft jazz," she said, eyes widening. "This is scary."

"You too?"

"My favorites."

"Lady A? Pink? Suzy Boggess? Beth Nielsen Chapman, Kacey Musgrave?" I asked.

"Oh shit. All of them."

"Damn," I said. A woman with a catholic taste in music. "OK, a tough one," I said. "Avett Brothers or Mumford & Son?"

"Mumford and Son are Avett Brothers wannabes," Carolyn said with conviction. "You?"

"You pegged it," I said.

"I lost all my music when I tossed my cell phone. I miss my tunes."

"Take the debit card, open an account under Madison and start downloading," I said.

"Great idea," she said, and for the next couple of hours, she was obsessed with downloading music.

"You really like the music I like?" she asked.

"Yes."

"Freaky."

***

Over the rest of the day's driving, I learned she was lost without Facebook and having withdrawal because of it. When I got tired and put her under the wheel, I discovered Carolyn couldn't drive for shit, she liked to talk with her hands while driving, look up at her hair, reapply lipstick and in general scare the hell out of anyone riding with her. I discovered it safer for my psyche to drive myself.

Another thing I knew but had reinforced, when a woman gets tired and whiny, no matter how pretty, it still makes a long trip that much longer. After 10 hours on the road, she was getting snappy. The constant sniping back and forth told me it was time to stop. We chose a Hampton Inn outside Mobile, going through a drive-through for dinner and eating in the room.

We had an ample supply of leftover booze and we started on the Long Island Teas again, with a similar result. I realized that she gets horny when she's had some drinks, which was fabulous because I do too.

This time the lovemaking was hurried, quick, and still fantastic. As we lay there with the overhead fan cooling our sweaty bodies, I felt my emotional wall giving way. I was enjoying her company too much, and my mind was fast forwarding me into daydreams that I had no place going.

Chapter 43

We had not moved in long minutes, two people who only days ago had been strangers, now locked together in an embrace—and a life or death struggle over a sword. It intensified things in my mind.

"You don't play much poker, do you?" Carolyn asked.

"No. I'm not very good at it."

"I know. You can't hide your emotions. I can read you. You are not a practiced liar."

"Is that good or bad," I asked.

"Depends on the profession, the intent, and the person. On you it's cute."

"Cute, huh?" I smiled.

"Oh, you were waiting for that one, weren't you?"

"You say I am not good at lying, so I'm not going to say anything."

"You are saying more than you know."

"You think? What am I saying that I'm not saying?"

Carolyn looked at me with a strange look, a little wistful, a little sad, maybe even a hint of what could have been but could never be. Her eyes watered but no tears. "You may have your focus, but you are getting some attachment to me."

"I like you."

"I know, I like you too. But it's more than that. And I've warned you about me. You do not want to do that. You can't get emotionally attached." She said. "You can't do that."

"It's not your choice," I said, adding under my breath, "Nor has it ever been my choice on whom I have ever become attached to. It's always been out of my control."

"You don't know me. I'm not the kind of person that deserves any emotion."

"Like I said, not your call. I can be emotional over whoever I choose. You can't stop me."

"Even if that emotion is not returned?" Carolyn asked.

"That has nothing to do with it. It is not like it is anything I can control. I didn't say it had to make sense or that you would understand. I do know that is how I am. I'm not saying it is one of my stronger traits."

"I'm warning you. Don't fall in love with me."

"Liking and feeling some emotional attachment is not love," I said.

"Depends on who you are talking to." My blank stare brought a sigh.

"OK, I am going to give you a dose of honesty. This is a two-drink story," she said. "I want this up front before things go any further. If you really want to hear it?"

"Carolyn," I said, locking gazes with her. "If I'm going to die in this endeavor, I want to know it all. I deserve that much."

"Yes, you do. It's not pretty," she said and began.

"Go ahead."

"As I said, we moved beside my Grandparents, and they raised us. It took with me. Their values, how I should live. It didn't take with Thomas.

"I was 16; he was 25 and already dealing with drugs from Mexico. One of his partners was/is Manuel Azeveda. He was the son of a big smuggler then. He came to visit my brother and I was at my brother's place in town and met him. He liked me. He liked me a lot, and what the hell does a 16-year-old know? I liked the attention. He made a big fuss over me.

"Manuel invited me to his hacienda in Mexico, and I was flirting, as much as I knew how in response to the attention. I didn't make any promises, but it was implied that I would go to visit with my brother's blessing.

"After he left Thomas explained to me that I was expected to go, and I would be expected to sleep with him and continue to sleep with him until he tired of me and moved on to someone else. 'That's the way they do it down there, and I need that kind of connection to him. He's going to be very big someday,' my brother said.

"I may have been 16 but I had enough sense to realize that my own brother was trying to whore me out to a Mexican drug dealer for his business interests. I told Grandad. It didn't go well."

"I can imagine," I said.

"Grandad handled it like Arizona ranchers have since the first Anglo went into that country. He took a shotgun and stuck it in Thomas' mouth and said if he ever came on the ranch again, ever made any attempt to try something like he had suggested, that his brains would be splattered all to hell and he would have a shallow grave out in the desert where the buzzards would pick his bones. Grandson or not. Thomas knew he meant it—and gave Manuel a warning to give me and Grandad a wide berth."

"I like your Grandad."

"You would have liked him. I see some similarities," she said.

"After that I had a couple of serious boyfriends in high school, both declaring love to get into my pants and I believed them and let them.

"My first boyfriend threw me over as soon as he had me, the second boyfriend was more serious, I thought I loved him, but it was more his infatuation with sex, and when he started college we were too far apart.

"I didn't speak to my brother again until he brought me a gift. It was a car, and it turned my head."

"A car?"

"Well, it was a jeep actually. I loved it. It was so cute. Thomas came to Grandad and apologized and convinced Grandad that he had changed. I helped. I convinced my Grandad to let me move in with Thomas for the last half of my senior year, and I was so insistent that Grandad gave in. Thomas was not much of a guardian, I went wild.

"I started at University of Texas, and that was when I realized that everyone saw me as above-average pretty. I became aware of the boys stumbling into things when I was around, following me, the cocky jocks making runs at me. Again, I liked the attention.

"I was complimented but I could see through it. I learned how to dress to encourage attention, what flirty things to say that other girls might not, just to watch their reaction and be a little nastier than the sorority girls.

"I was flirty but more serious than the girls in the sororities. I dated a few guys but nothing too deep, just fun for a night out type of thing. I wasn't a party girl." She paused, "And some guys got lucky if I wanted them to and they were nice about it."

Carolyn paused, taking a deep breath, obvious this revealing of herself was tough for her.

"At the start of my senior year in college, I had just turned 21, one of my room mates told me about her part-time job. She was a waitress at the Yellow Rose, a strip club in Austin. Even though she kept her clothes on, she said she was making $200 a night in tips, and bet I could make even more, so I tried it. My first night I made $300, wearing this tiny little outfit that pushed up my boobs and made them look huge and a low back that showed off half my ass. We learned quickly to kneel down when putting drinks on a table rather than bend over.

"One Friday night some older drunk guy wanted to see my tits. I told him no. He offered me $500 to see my tits."

"What did you do?"

"Are you crazy? I showed him for $500. One of the managers saw me and wanted me to fill in as a stripper; he was short on dancers that night, so that was a start and for six months I stripped. I loved the attention. It was interesting; the power a woman has over a man when you get your bare boobs down in their face.

"In the middle of a club it is not like anything untoward is going to happen other than a guy copping a quick feel—and that makes the tip a lot better. I had no problem letting a guy get a good feel for a nice tip.

"The VIP room at the Yellow Rose is a raised area still part of the main room, so it is not like there is any hanky panky going on there either. All in all, it was a nice place to work."

"Why did you quit?" I asked.

"Two things. One customer got obsessed with me. I gave him my number so he could call me when he was in town so I would be sure to be working that night—but he took it further than that. It got to the point I felt he was almost stalking me. He called so much I refused to answer the phone and had to change my number. I asked him to stop calling. He showed up at the club a couple of times after that and it freaked me out.

"The next time he asked for me, I refused to sit with him. He tried to get me in trouble with the manager, but Liam was a nice guy and took my side, told the customer he could get dances from someone else or he could leave. The last time he came back in he was already drunk and made a scene and they threw him out, banned him from the club."

"And the second reason?"

"My last night there was when a guy came in and said they were filming a cheap budget movie outside of Round Rock and offered me a walk-on role. He was going to put me in the movies. I quit that night."

"And the movie?"

"A bomb, you have never heard of it. But I had made my way to the silver screen. I didn't finish my senior year. I went to Hollywood chasing fame and fortune. I kept chasing but never caught it."

"What happened?" I asked. "It is not like you lack anything in looks."

"Thank you, but I do by Hollywood standards. It took me a few years to figure it out, but there were several reasons why my acting plan wasn't working. I mean I went to the auditions and tried not to be discouraged. I did land a couple of small parts and one TV commercial, but I had no formal acting training. More than once I was told I was pretty, but I didn't know how to act.

"They were right. I'd gotten most of what I wanted by being pretty. There everyone was pretty."

"Sounds like you are too tough on yourself," I said.

"The other reason is after seeing what had happened to my brother, I wouldn't touch drugs, and coke was the social thing at all the parties. If you didn't indulge, they thought something was wrong with you, or you were snitching, and you might be a narc or something. And the final thing was I would not suck cock or fuck to get a call-back for an audition. This was before all this Me-Too movement started. Some producers and directors demanded sexual things, others expected it. You would be amazed at the big names that got their names out there by the quality of their blow jobs. Hell, I think it is a joke that Harvey Weinstein got singled out. I know big name guys guilty of much worse."

"OK," I said, still following.

"I took some modeling jobs part-time to earn living expenses, advertising stuff mostly, then they said my hips were too big, they wanted skinny bony girls that looked like teenagers and I was getting older. I got tired of being a human clothes hanger for the photos. It stopped being fun.

"I went to Santa Barbara to get some acting courses, finish up my degree, and then went back to LA for another try. It didn't go much better than the first time, a couple of better parts. One featured me in a nude scene in which I show my boobs that you can find on all the celebrity nude sites if you know where to look. One producer wanted me with larger boobs, even offered to pay for them and guaranteed the role. I passed.

"Then I met Joseph. By this point in my life, I realized I was not going to be the next Meryl Streep or Olivia Wilde, and Joseph had reached the same conclusion on his side of the business. We collided and joined in our shared disillusionment.

"We lived together a year, then married, and while we thought we loved each other and professed it, and we did love each other a little, but not enough, you know? We were good friends and lovers, not necessarily good spouses. He cheated and had a propensity for young girls. I cheated a few times with some local guys in Santa Barbara more for revenge than desire. Then he died. I never really realized how much I loved him until he died.

"I went into a long tailspin brought on by grief. I had a couple of friends that were trying to help me through it, but nothing helped. Then slowly I began to get better, at least to the point I could live with myself. But I learned I will never open myself to that kind of pain again. Love can do that to you."

"Yes, it can," I said.

Carolyn half guffawed. "You say that like you've been there."

"I have," stealing a line from her. "If you want to hear it."

"We have nothing but time," she said. "Go on." I gave her a 10-minute version of my life with Carolyn III.

Carolyn said nothing for a long time after I finished. "The bitch gutted you, huh?"

"Pretty much."

"Well, we have that in common. But here you are getting an old tingle again, this time toward me?"

"Maybe a little tingle," I admitted.

"You've been warned," she said. "I don't know what else to say. I've admitted enough about me that it should scare you away."

"You say you read me pretty well," I said.

"Yes."

"Look in my eyes." She did. "What do you see? Do I look like I am the kind of person that scares away easily?"

"No. There a coldness in your eyes that scares me a little."

"I know. It scares me sometimes too."

"Maybe that's why I know you can protect me," she said, snuggling against me as I pulled the sheet over us. "But you have been warned."

"Yes, I have."

Chapter 44

The next day the traveling was better. Less whining from my traveling companion, and anticipation that we were at least closing in on a possible potential buyer.

"I've been wondering," I said. "When your brother asked for the sword, knowing how he was, and he offered to buy it, why didn't you sell it to him."

"Because he would have never paid me," she said. "It would not be the first time."

"Still..."

"And I need the money. Joseph's life insurance money is what I'm living on. It is almost gone. We are upside down in the house, I have no movie roles, I'm too old for the big money modeling, and just about too old to go back to stripping. I'm running out of options. I don't want a sugar daddy either."

Carolyn said it in a matter of fact manner that told me she considered that as a serious option. The outburst left me saying only a soft, "Oh."

***

As we continued out I-10 we hit the long Basin Bridge over the swamp and bayou between Baton Rouge and Breaux Bridge. "You remember when we left Huntington and I was talking about pretty places in this country?"

"Look to your left in a minute, we are crossing Whiskey Bay right now. You'll see it when we get to

Henderson." We hit the coffee table book view of the cypress knees and glimmering water.

"Wow, that's beautiful." She was seeing the glistening expanse of water as far as the eye could see, with no evidence of humans save for a houseboat tied to the left and two men in the distance in a bass boat.

"It's the Atchafalaya Basin."

"Something about it pulls you, doesn't it?" She said. "I've love to be out there on it."

"My thoughts exactly," I said.

"Thanks for keeping me from looking down at my phone when we got here, I would have hated to have missed it." She said as the view faded. She looked back down at her phone. I smiled.

***

After a half hour of silence and smooth jazz on the radio, I told her, "Talk to me. I'm getting sleepy."

"Want me to drive?" she volunteered.

"No, just talk to me."

"OK, what about?"

"Anything. You say you learned to read men, in the strip club?"

"Oh yeah, it was great training for that. A pair of bare boobs can turn most men into jelly," she laughed.

"Guilty," I said. "That's why I put three dancers through college," I said. She gave me a strange look. "At least that's what they said they were doing with that money."

Carolyn laughed. "Yeah, I would have made a lot of money off you."

"Yes, you probably would have," I said. "And money well spent."

"You must have some great stories," I said.

"Only three that come to mind."

"I have nothing but highway time," I said.

***

"My first story is not much of a story," Carolyn said. "Desiree had a baby, took some time off, got back into shape quick and was still breastfeeding. She was never that big but with the milk-enhanced boobs, she was proud of them and worked wearing a loose sheer top. She got a lot of attention that way, and one night she was sitting on a customer's lap, but she wasn't drinking anything but water. She finished her water and felt the milk building up; it was time for a feeding or using a breast pump."

"OK."

"But she had a paying customer there too, the kid was with the sitter, she didn't have a breast pump. So, she asks the customer if breast milk offends him. He says no. She puts the empty water bottle up to her nipple, squeezes her boob and squirts her breast milk into the water bottle, milking herself."

"No."

"Yes. The customer looked a little weirded out, but he was game, going along, but Bret, the bouncer, who played football at UT and worked security part time had never been exposed to what breasts were made for—and he freaked, I mean came unglued freaked out. He was screaming. He made Desiree go into the dressing room.

"You can't do that in here," he screamed. "Everyone in the place was howling in laughter, not at Desiree but at Bret's reaction."

"I can say I never saw anything like that before," I said. "That the strangest thing you ever saw?"

"No. I was working a day shift on a Friday, a businessman in a suit had taken a four-martini lunch and was so drunk his buddies left him, and there weren't many people there. A new girl, a tall brunette with really long legs came out on stage in this red sequined sling swimsuit with matching red sequined shoes—with these big long spike heels."

"Ruby Red slippers?"

"No, just sexy red stripper pole climbers," Carolyn said. "She has her top off, the drunk businessman staggers to the dollar rail and holds out a five. She leans over and dangles these big boobs in his face, and I guess he figured since there are not many people there that no one would care if he copped a feel, so he reaches up both hands and starts fondling and squeezing.

"The girl on stage screams, straightens up, leans on one leg and kicks out with the other foot, hitting the businessman in his upper chest with that spike high heel. He falls to the floor with that red sequined heel stuck in his chest.

"The paramedics arrive, treat him right there on the floor, put him on a stretcher and roll him out—with that bright red shoe still stuck in his breastbone. I always wondered how he explained that one to his wife."

***

"Well I've always tried to be a gentleman to dancers," I said.

"Been a while, hasn't it?"

"How do you know?"

"I told you I can read you like a book now," she grinned, but continued, "No one calls strippers dancers anymore—they are called entertainers now."

"In other words, less dancing,"

"And a whole lot more grinding on a lap, yes," Carolyn said.

As we rode down the highway, I glanced over at her and she had unbuttoned three buttons on her blouse, the teasing way she leaned over gave me an unobstructed view of her right breast. She would look clothed to anyone on the right side of the car. She saw me looking. "You like?"

"What's not to like."

"If you start running out of the road I'll button up."

"I'm a safe driver."

"And you are wondering why I did that, huh?" she asked.

"It did cross my mind."

"I'm proving to you I can read you. You said you were a boob man."

"Yes, I am."

"Then you are loving this, and I'm keeping you from getting sleepy," she smiled. "I told you, I've been a stripper, nudity doesn't bother me."

"Your nudity doesn't bother me either," I smiled. "I like it."

"I knew you would," she said.

"Your effort is not wasted; I am no longer sleepy. You said you had three stories?"

"Yes, the last story also influenced my quitting.

There was this one guy who came in all the time, we called him Chicken Man because he supplied the chicken for the Great Texas Taco company, whose worldwide headquarters is in Austin. He would come in regularly from Georgia to keep things flowing smoothly for his supplying the taco company."

"They're big, they are even in the supermarket in Huntington," I said.

"They are international, and it is a lot of chicken. He had a ton of chicken houses and brokered for some other chicken farmers too—and he had money to burn. He had the hots for Alana, this tall German girl who had done some fashion modeling, beautiful girl, cute accent, and the Chicken man was smitten.

"He came to Austin about once a month for two or three days, and he was at the Yellow Rose every time he was there, lavishing money on Alana. He was one of those white knights.

"Like you were saying about me, a good guy?"

"An entertainer's definition of a white knight is a guy who comes in and is taken in by a girl's looks, and his first thought is to take her away from all the sin and iniquity. If he can't do that he can at least provide as much business as possible so someday she can escape this grind. But he never understands that a lot of the girls are there because they can make a lot of money for showing their boobs and it is easy work compared to a lot of other jobs, and her interest in him is all about money. No entertainer in her right mind seriously dates a customer.

"After the first night of walking around with no top, it is never the same again. Your modesty goes away, and you never think a thing about your nudity in a room of clothed men. A white knight doesn't see it that she is enjoying it, making good money. Instead, he wants to save her from herself.

"One trick that you can always pull on a white knight who is dropping serious money and is getting ready to go, but you want to keep the cash flowing a little longer, you point out some ugly guy walking into the club. You tell the white knight, 'Hey there's that awful guy that I can't stand, he's rude, grabby, and I hate to have to sit with him, he has horrible breath, but he always asks for me. Do me a favor and hang around a while and let me keep sitting with you and maybe he will leave me alone tonight.' The reality is you don't have a clue who the guy at the door even is. You may never have seen him before, but the white knight doesn't know that he just digs deeper for the cash to save you."

"And you see me like that?" I asked. I didn't see being gullible as a compliment.

"In ways, but in good ways," she laughed. "If you were a white knight in a club, you'd never get to sleep with me, it spoils my image of you. Now if the valet asks me out and he's cute, that's something else."

"Well, that is good to know," I said. "Now about the Chicken man."

"So, he is focused on Alana, thinks he is in love, and Alana is playing along. It gets to the point that he starts wanting her to go back to Georgia to the chicken farm with him. And she never says yes, but never says no, always coming up with an excuse, and the Chicken man kept pouring out the money."

"Why do I feel like this is going to end badly?" I asked.

"Don't get ahead of me," Carolyn said. "It comes to a head when one night the Chicken man has had enough. He tells Alana that the bullshit has gone on long enough. She can quit teasing and go back with him to Georgia and the chicken farm that night like she said she would, or he would never come back in again. He shows her two plane tickets, one in his name, and one in hers.

"In an effort to stall, Alana tells him, 'I would love to go with you, but I have 35,000 dollars in debt, and I must keep working to pay it off. Until I get that paid off, I cannot consider going with you.'

"The Chicken man asks for a check from her bank. She tears it out and hands it to him and he goes to the quiet area of the club. They have small spaces like old phone booths where you can get in and close the door and be able to hear on your cell phone over the sound system in the club. He makes a few calls. When he comes back, he asks her if she has online banking on her phone. She tells him, yes, and he tells her to check her balance. She does. The Chicken man has put 35 grand into her account."

"What?"

"Yes, 35 big ones. Alana has no excuses now; she must say yes. The Chicken man is ecstatic, and he tells her he's ready to go right now. She says she needs to pack, so she goes into the dressing room, removes her dancing costume and changes into street clothes, gets into a cab with the Chicken man and packs two suitcases at her apartment while he waits in the living room.

"About the time she's finished, the phone rings. Her best friend is in a car accident, she needs Alana at the hospital right now. Alana tells the Chicken man to take her bags on with him, check them with his stuff and she will get the ticket changed and be on tomorrow.

"The Chicken man leaves with her two bags, going home to his chicken farm awaiting Alana's arrival. What he doesn't know is Alana recruited her friend when she went to change clothes to give her a call 20 minutes later with the car wreck story.

"Alana had filled her two oldest suitcases with a stack of clothes she had laid out for the Goodwill. The next day she goes to the airport, cashes in the ticket, and decides it might be a good time to leave Austin, 35 grand to the good."

"Damn," I said. "That is cold."

"I'm not through yet," Carolyn said. "Alana goes to Florida and dances there for about a year, comes back to Austin to visit friends and decides to work a shift at the club. She is on stage when in walks the Chicken man. He sees her, walks straight up to her on the stage and puts a 100-dollar bill in her garter. 'I don't know what went wrong last year,' he says, 'but I'm sorry. Can we start over?'

"Alana got off stage, went out the back door, and never went back. I know because I was in LA by then and she crashed with me for a week before she found a job dancing at the Spearmint Rhino."

"That's all true?" I asked.

"Every bit of it. I thought it was cold too, treating a man that way, but he wanted to be a white knight, so he did deserve a little of it. It woke me up though, to the kind of world I was working that someone I called a friend would do that to a customer."

"You called me a white knight," I said.

"You're comparing apples and oranges," she said. "You are a different kind of white knight."

"How so?"

Carolyn leaned over and gave me a kiss. "Because you are my white knight."

Chapter 45

"Five million dollars? You've lost your fucking mind Max." Briscoe Reddix was screaming. I had dealt with him before, I knew some of it was put-on, some of it was sticker shock, and none of it because he didn't want the sword. It was right up his alley.

Briscoe was right out of a book about how a West Texas oilman would dress. Immaculate straw hat, ramrod straight back, white shirt under a western cut jacket, jeans that had been laundered and starched so much there was a straight white line at both creases, ending in exotic leather handmade boots. The ones he wore today were fine grain Ostrich skin, handmade. Mercedes del Rio, it looked like from the distinctive cut.

"You have a chance to own the rarest sword in the world. The most famous word in history, the sword of the shoguns. It's worth 10 times that if I could put it up at auction."

"Yeah, I know you're right," he admitted. "I'd like to have it, but it is too rich for my blood." I looked around the room. We were behind a vault door adjoining his office, with a wall full of Henry and Yellow Boy Winchesters, some of which dated back to the time when his great grandfather had settled the area and were the arsenal rifles he had bought for the ranch hands to fight off rustlers and hostile Indians.

There was a bank of drawers all around the room, filled with Western collectibles from spurs to knives, sheriff badges to single action Army Colts. He owned one of Custer's 7th Cavalry's issue pistols and had been trying to buy Custer's ivory-handled Colts that Libby Custer had owned.

"So you gonna pass on the rarest sword in the world?"

"Have to," Briscoe said. "Oil's way down."

"Know anyone else?" I asked.

"My boy Damon might know, he's a cop in Del Rio but on the side, he's been buying and selling some antiques down in Old Mexico. A lot of money down there right now if you don't care where it comes from," he said. "Nice thing about cash. Once you get it in your hand the money doesn't have a memory—it is yours now."

"I've heard that," I said, giving Carolyn a sideways glance. She rolled her eyes. "We do not care where the money comes from."

"Why don't you two hang around for a couple of days and let me see what I can dig up?" he said. He was staring straight at Carolyn as he said it. He was obvious.

"Bullshit, Briscoe," I said. "You just want me to hang around, so you can stare at Carolyn here a little more. Besides, I have a couple of contacts I have to see in San Antone."

"If I was 20 years younger, I'd do a hell of a lot more than just stare, you can count on that." He looked at me, up and down. "Don't know how you do it, you asshole, but you do come up with some fine-looking women."

"Must be something unseen," I laughed.

"Nah, that's not it at all," Carolyn tossed in, grinning at Briscoe. He moved over to her and wrapped his arm around her waist, smiling. She leaned into him. He liked her reaction.

"I like this one, Max. You better not let her get away. I might go after her despite being 20 years too old."

"Be careful, Mr. Reddix, I might just slow down and let you catch me if Max runs me off."

Reddix roared. "Hell girl, you'd kill me, but I'd die happy."

I gave Briscoe my new cell number and we turned back toward San Antonio. I had a room at the Hyatt and dinner planned for the Rhine Mein Steak House.

We checked in, going for the cheaper room, the one with the view of the Alamo rather than the Riverwalk. I didn't go into my usual tirade with the check-in rep about how fundamentally charging less for a view of the historic Alamo, but before we went to dinner Carolyn did have to listen to my version of those 13 days of glory at the siege of the Alamo.

"I went to school in Texas, I know about it," she said.

"OK, who survived?"

"That's easy. Jim Bowie's slave, and Captain Dickenson's wife and daughter."

"Their names?"

Carolyn could only come up with one. "Susannah," she said.

"Right, the wife. Now the daughter?"

"I can't."

"Do you know what happened to them?"

"No, but I bet you are going to tell me," Carolyn said.

"I am. They both ended up working as whores in Galveston. The daughter, Angelia, died first."

"Damn, why don't you try to cheer me up," Carolyn deadpanned. She listened to the rest of my descriptions.

We walked the ground. I pointed out where Davy Crockett's waist-high wall was defended and where the men in the long barracks waited for their last shot while the Mexican troops loaded the cannon and blew in each barracks door before the troops rushed in to finish off the defenders.

I had made this walk with others. This time what was different, Carolyn listened and seemed to understand. She teared up.

Chapter 46

Daniel had come through with my San Antonio lead the day before I stopped at Briscoe's. He was my only meeting, although I told Briscoe I had two to put some pressure on his decision. In the end, he didn't bite and passed, so it was on to San Antonio.

"Shinichi Wantanabe" Daniel said. "Big buyer and collector, he's on a buying tour. Stopped in this afternoon. He buys for a lot of the Japanese wealthy families," Daniel said. "I mentioned your name in a couple of other places, but nothing has turned up."

"Give him my number," I said.

In less than an hour, I received a text from Watanabe. "I'm told you have a rare Japanese sword. Would like to see it. Can we meet?"

"We can," I said. "San Antonio day after tomorrow. Outside the Alamo at 3 p.m. Can you be here?"

"I can," came the reply. "I am not that far away; I will be in Dallas tomorrow."

An hour later Briscoe called. "I have a name for you," he said. "Alamando Ruiz. Here's his number in Mexico. He's got deep pockets and he likes the very good stuff. I didn't tell him what you have though." I gave Briscoe's lead a call and invited him to meet outside the Alamo the next day as well. At 7 p.m.

Something in my gut felt uneasy, a sensation I have learned to trust. I didn't want to do this meet without backup. My last call was to Allen back in Carolina, instructing him to catch the first plane out and be here by tomorrow, even if he had to charter something.

"It looks like we are rolling," I said. "Before you get on the plane, I need you to make a side stop in Atlanta for me though," I explained what I had in mind.

"No problem," he said. "I'll have to fly out of there anyway. I'll only have to leave a little earlier. I'll text you my flight times."

Carolyn was excited as she jumped into my arms as I entered the hotel room. "I think this is going to work. And I liked your friend Briscoe. I wonder if you will be like that when you get old?"

"What do you mean?"

"You know, fun."

"You mean I'm not that way now?"

"You know what I mean."

"Oh, horny like Briscoe. Yes, I'm like that right now."

"Then do something about it, big boy," she challenged. And I did.

***

It was a quiet moment in the afterglow of two glorious rounds of romping with the most beautiful woman I had ever known. Heaven. She was snuggling under my arm. The wall that she let down sometimes for a few moments in the throes of lovemaking was back up. I did not know when our time together like this would end, but my gut told me it would be soon, very soon if the sword sale got resolved quickly. I was regretting that moment even before it was in sight and for a moment even wondered if there was some way to drag it out a little longer to extend my time with her.

Reality hit me quicker though because I knew there was only so long that we could keep running without making a slip-up or simply being unlucky and our pursuers catching up. As I lay there, I kept mentally replaying our moves, backtracking to see if we made any mistakes.

Live for the moment, today is all you have, I kept telling myself. If things did not go as planned, living for the moment is the best I could do.

"If we pull this off, what are you going to do after?" I asked.

"Go back to Santa Barbara, pay the house off, put the rest in the bank and watch the ocean."

"Not much of a career move," I said.

"I wouldn't be in porn, that's the primary outlet for actresses like me who can't make it in real film. And the age window is closing on that."

"That business seems to take the very best of a woman, gobble her up, and toss her back out on the street before they are 40."

"In all but a few cases, that's right."

"You are still young outside the entertainment field." She ignored the statement.

"What about you?" she asked.

"I'm going back to my Carolina mountains and pay it on my debts...as far as it will go."

"Really?" She missed the joke entirely.

"OK, my idea of bliss, I enjoy what I do, buying and selling. It allows me to play with high-end collectibles that I could never own and put away like normal collectors. Collecting is going away eventually, this new generation has no interest it, but I want to do that as long as I can. Doing it long term as a continuing career is a real long shot, but then again, I've always been a sucker for a long shot," I said.

"Hopefully, by the time that collecting runs its course I can retire, or maybe get into something else," I continued. "Real estate is good there, a lot of tourists come in wanting summer homes, things like that. I like meeting new people, a couple of friends have agencies I could work for, which might be fun."

"I wasn't talking about a career," Carolyn said. "Everyone wants a career. The problem comes when there is no chance of a career that you wanted, like me."

"OK. I want a ski-boat and a pontoon. Not all at once, but when my kids get away from their bitch of a Momma, I am going to reestablish myself with them, and I am going to need the boats to entertain my grandchildren."

"I sometimes wish Joseph and I had had a kid or two. I was afraid it would mess up my figure then, I had enough things working against my career at the time—he didn't want the commitment. A good thing looking back on it, but still, I do wonder. A kid might give me a bona fide reason to exist, a goal, to see them grow up and thrive."

"That's every parent's goal," I said, but "Woulda, coulda, shoulda."

"Yeah, living life is a real bitch sometimes."

"Let's hope it just gets better." I felt Carolyn's hand reaching between my legs, and then lowering her head down I heard her say before I felt her on me.

"Well in some ways it just got better for you didn't it?"

"Damn right."

Chapter 47

Allen arrived by lunch and I spread my arsenal from the SUV on the bed before him. "Take your pick," I said. He chose the Glock .40 from my bug-out bag, along with the standard magazine and two more 15 rounders. He raised his pants leg over his prosthesis, unsnapped a compartment where his calf would be, placed my Daniel Winkler dagger inside and closed it back, replacing his pants leg. "Damn near forgot the dagger I normally carry there when I was heading for the plane this morning," he laughed. "Had to go back to the car and put the knife under the seat."

"Hopefully you won't need any of that today."

"I just stand to the side nondescript and keep everyone safe, that it? That the plan?"

"That's it," I said.

"Seems simple enough," he said. "But you know what they say about plans."

"Yeah, they only exist until the first shot's fired. Let's hope none of that will happen here."

"And how is home?" I asked.

Allen laughed, "Vernon was checking on your place, put up a couple of game cameras and discovered you had a couple of visitors waiting on your return, taking shifts hiding in the bushes. They were not the ones that beat up Terry, he said."

I smiled. "OK, what did Vernon do?"

"Seems like someone shot the tires out of their vehicle during a shift change. They've not been back again."

"Vernon messing with the tourists again," I said. I didn't mention that someone was expending a lot of resources looking for us.

***

Watanabe was on time, as I expected. It was hard to miss the small oriental man in the midst of the bustling tourists. I introduced myself with a bow and extended my business card, the info in Japanese facing him, the English side down. He handed his to me the same way, and I gave him the courtesy of studying it before sliding it into a pocket. Understanding Japanese customs as well, Carolyn stood further back but close at hand.

"Tell me about your valuable sword," Watanabe said.

"First I must be assured of your absolute confidentially," I said.

"Always. Our reputation attests to that."

I handed him the photos of the hamon line. At the third photograph he looked up, his hands shaking. He recognized what we were offering. "Oh my. Oh my. Oh my. Is…Is it...Is it?"

I nodded my head. "A war trophy," I said. "And you have the opportunity to return it home. Discreetly."

"Yes, yes. Discreet very important, his excited accent making it come out 'belly belly important'." He glanced down at the photos again. It was the Holy Grail to any sword aficionado. It would be a once in a lifetime achievement to return a National Treasure back to Japan, even if no one in the public knew. The important people in Japan would know—it was too important to not let a quiet word slip here and there. Once it got back into Japanese hands no one would want to ask how it had gotten back home, the fact it was there would be enough.

"Real?"

"You have the photos. What do you think?"

"Nice. Belly Belly nice. You have here, now?"

"No. It is in a safe place. It will only be shown to serious potential customers."

"I am serious. I would like to see."

"The price is 20 million."

"Ahhh soooo." He nodded. The amount did not startle him. "OK. I would like to see. When?" I motioned Carolyn over.

"'Fess up time girl. He wants to see the sword. He is serious."

"Three days. We will send the location."

I looked up and that was when I noticed the two heavyset Japanese men in thick sports jackets in the shade of the nearby wall. I could see the bulge under their jackets tell me both were carrying large caliber handguns in shoulder holsters. Behind them 10 feet, his hand in his dispatch bag was Allen, staring at their backs. He lifted his eyebrows to signal he was on them should things get hinky.

Watanabe walked away saying he would remain in San Antonio pending my notification. The two bodyguards followed a few feet behind, and they went down the steps by the waterfall toward the Riverwalk.

I took Carolyn to "The Price of Freedom" film at the IMAX. Allen followed and sat two rows behind. After a drink on the Riverwalk, we went back to the front of the Alamo to meet our second prospect.

***

Alamando Ruiz was not happy to learn there was another buyer in play. He too did not flinch at the 20-million-dollar price tag. He also was given a time of three days until examination, with the location to be announced.

Ruiz had a couple of friends watching his back too, as my friend Allen watched theirs. There was a reason I was meeting these two potential customers in one of the most public places in Texas.

***

Allen slept in the room next door that night. I could feel things were ending, and I was trying to cram as much love making time with Carolyn as I could, and I wanted the privacy.

Carolyn was a different woman making love, utilizing positions, whispers, touches, and seductions that I would have never dreamed. She executed each naturally, always with the right whisper or naughty suggestion in perfect timing with my body's desire. Maybe it was natural, maybe it was experience, but I didn't care.

This woman turned me inside out, both physically and emotionally. My effort to distance my emotions from her had failed, and I knew it. The more time with her, the more of her I enjoyed, the more I wanted, even knowing as soon as we were finished, before the afterglow had faded, her wall would be back up and her emotional distance would be back in place. I knew she could see my growing attachment. She was too savvy to miss it, but she stopped pushing me away, even if she was not returning the encouragement I coveted.

I was facing the reality that all this would end and if I were lucky, I would be back in a small mountain town with nothing left of this adventure but memories and a few bucks. That was more than I had when I started, but it was not all I wanted.

In the long run, all we can really hope to have in our old age are some descendants who love us and memories of the good times—hopefully enough to crowd out the bad times. The problem on this deal is the potential for bad times far outweighed the potential for good—if we lived to enjoy it.

I was haunted by the image of the ambush of the two police officers at Carolyn's Santa Barbara house and how professionally they had done it. We were not dealing with amateurs. Allen and I were civilians now, no longer employed by our government in making our nation's enemies die for the politician's ideology. We knew war, and we had stared down death before, but the obvious difference between them and us was the cartel hit team enjoyed the killing.

Chapter 48

The next morning, packed and ready to go, I left Allen with Carolyn while I went to retrieve the Expedition. I was in the parking deck headed toward the SUV when I found my way blocked by two men, one tall with a hawk face. They were presenting a dilemma.

***

True to the F.B.I. statistics, the entire gunfight lasted only a few seconds. Three shots, three seconds, but rather than three feet as in the 3-3-3 rule, the distance was more like eight to ten feet. There was no time for thought or aim, but there was plenty of time for one man dead and the other dying, handguns in their hand.

I figured most of what just happened was probably on security film. Justifiable self-defense—but only after a lot of paperwork, bullshit, and publicity. None of which I wanted, and I could not afford to be in a police interview room at a time when our pursuers had found us and no one protecting Carolyn. I didn't know how our pursuers found us but that did not matter now. They had. What mattered now was escape.

The two men braced me in the deck close to the elevators, before I got close to the Expedition, so with the vehicle out of the video I thought we could still retrieve it and drive away—but I knew better than to have my image getting into that vehicle inside the parking deck.

I stepped into the elevator, puked in the alley beside the parking deck, and called Allen with hurried instructions to meet me in the lobby, where I did a brush pass with the keys.

Carolyn and I rolled our bags on the street to the corner near the Buckhorn Saloon where we met Allen, who had retrieved the Expedition. The rear door had not completed risen before I was tossing bags in and we loaded. We were entering the traffic and were turning at the corner when the first black and white turned into the deck a block away. The unit was at full tilt with flashing lights and siren. Other sirens echoed in the distance.

While he drove, I disassembled the Glock I had used, popped off the serial number plate, each piece going into a different trash container every block or two. I held the number plate, barrel and firing pin until we were going over a river and consigned them to the mud there.

As we left San Antonio I turned on the news, watching the helicopters all heading toward the Riverwalk. "Breaking news," one of the broadcasters said. "We are following a mass shooting at a parking deck near the Riverwalk. A total of five people dead." Allen and I exchanged glances. "The announcer continued. "One of the dead has been identified as a Japanese diplomat Shinichi Watanabe, his two bodyguards, and two others. The fatalities were found in the parking deck of the Hyatt hotel and in two rooms of the hotel. We have been told terrorism is suspected but not totally ruled out at this time. Stand by for more. The area is in lockdown."

"Wasn't that the guy…" Allen said.

"Yes, that was the guy," I quoted Warren Zevon: "Send lawyers, guns, and money…"

"The shit has hit the fan." Allen finished the verse.

"What?" Carolyn asked from the back seat.

"We lost half our potential customers," I said, "And our pursuers are far too close. Stay alert," I cautioned

Allen, but then I did not have to say it; he was already on code yellow.

"We gotta get rid of this vehicle," Allen said. We pulled off and I started driving while he was punching in his cell phone.

"How in the hell did they find us?" Carolyn asked.

"And take out Watanabe and his two guys?" I said.

"Those guys watching Watanabe were pretty good too," Allen said. "They knew what they were doing. They would not have been easy to take down."

"Now what?"

"Now we go find a fucking sword. No more excuses. And we're going to have a meeting with your brother in Phoenix," I told Carolyn.

"Phoenix is on the way." Carolyn was pouting, for what reason I did not know for sure, maybe because we had lost the customer, maybe fear from the gunplay, or maybe even second-guessing her choice about what to do with the sword. "If you are so damn smart why don't we do that first," she said. "I'd love to see the look on Thomas' face if the people he is searching for turns up in his office."

And that is what we did.

Chapter 49

Carolyn knew the layout of her brother's company and gave us a good diagram ahead of time. There was a parking spot near the front door with a circular concrete platform boasting a fountain and the company logo in the center, so it was easy to pull up and be through the front door once we had passed the gate. We didn't stop for security; I slowed and gave him a wave of my hand like we knew we had business there. "We are late for an appointment with McMasters" I said as we passed. "Can't wait. Will sign in on the way out."

The guard looked confused but instead of calling anyone he nodded. I saw him lay the clipboard back down and retake his seat in the shade. The bluff had worked. In seconds we were through the front door. Not quite as fast an entrance as fast roping from a Blackhawk, but the old Gunny would have been proud of how quick we breached the building.

Inside and quick stepping we followed Carolyn's lead to find ourselves at the outer office of Thomas McMasters. We didn't wait to be announced and burst in through the door.

"What the..." He started to say more, but two things that stopped him. The sight of his sister and the pressure of a .40 cal. Glock I had shoved against his forehead.

"Sit the fuck back down and listen. I don't want to hear a damn thing you got to say. You've been looking for me and her, well by God, now, you have found us. I am going to tell you how this plays out. This shit ends now. Right now, this minute. If not, I am going to splatter your brains all over this office. Do you understand, motherfucker?"

I moved the pistol off his flesh, there was a round hole in the flesh where I had been pressing the gun barrel. I pushed the gun back against his head.

"Nod your head if you understand, and I said do not say a fucking word. Nod." He nodded.

"I do not give a flying fuck about your Japanese deal. It is no concern of ours. Good luck with that, but if you fuck with me anymore, or your sister, or interfere with her sword deal, I will be back and kill your fucking ass. Again, do you understand, motherfucker? Again, he nodded.

"Tell me you understand."

"I understand."

"Do you think I am joking? That I am bluffing?" He locked eyes with me. There was cold hollow darkness in them.

"No."

"Damn right," and I pistol-whipped him across the top of the head, and he tumbled half out of his chair. I tossed a box of tissue to him to slow the trickle of blood from the open scalp cut from my blow.

"Any police stop me, there will be a great news story in tomorrow's paper about the discovery of a stolen Japanese sword and I will say it was in your possession and was trying to get it back to the Japanese and you wanted to fuck with the Japanese, you understand? You can kiss your Japanese deal goodbye." Again, he nodded.

"I'm glad we understand each other." I looked over at Carolyn. "You have anything to add?"

"No, I think you about summed it up," she said with a sarcastic smile. Allen remained back against the wall, his hand in his pocket without speaking. I turned and stomped out of his office, Carolyn was right behind; Allen paused and gave Thomas a nod that he was a part of the threat before bringing up the rear.

"You know that meant nothing to him," she said. "He will not stop."

"It meant something to me," I said.

"What do you mean?"

"I've warned him. Next time I kill him. What happens next is on him."

***

Allen was driving and he turned into a shopping center parking lot down the street from the battery company office building, backing halfway into the space beside a small minivan. He parked, walked to the minivan and reached under the front fender, coming out with keys. He opened the side door of the minivan.

I didn't have to ask what was happening and I knew he would explain once we were rolling. We quickly offloaded the firearms from the security drawer, our bags, Allen's long duffle, and Allen stripped off the two dealer plates, tossing them in the back.

"Where did you get this van?" I asked.

"Traded it online while you were driving," he grinned. "I love these smartphones. I found a Phoenix car dealer on the internet that I have done business with before; I bought a 69 Mustang Coupe from him a while back. I checked this vehicle out online, read the CarFax, and we made the arrangements to do the deal here, as I told him I would be in a hurry."

"Where is he?"

"Waiting in the food court. He'll figure it out when he comes outside. I put the keys on the front tire, he knows to look there. The cash difference has already been paid. Paypal. Also, I checked it out; this is a blind spot in the mall's security camera."

"How did you do that?"

"I called the mall when we stopped for that bathroom break at Buckees. I told them I had been parked here two weeks ago, my car had been stolen, and security told me that I was in a part of the parking area that wasn't covered with cameras. I needed the name of the street because my insurance company was being balky without the specific address."

"How did you know they would have a blind spot?"

"They all have blind spots. Don't you read the papers?" Allen said.

"Great thinking," I said. "I knew I had you out here for something positive."

"Taking care of your worthless ass is what," Allen smiled.

"And you did all this over your phone?"

"I told the car dealer I was traveling. He said he'll wait three days before filing the title."

"Nice to have a good brother," I smiled at Carolyn.

"I wouldn't know. Remember, I just left mine." She said. "Why are we changing vehicles though?" Allen had his finger in one ear and was talking into the receiver in a low voice.

"If the guys from the parking garage put a tracking device in the Expedition, it is going to lead them to the mall closest to their partner. If Thomas calls the cops, they will be looking for the Expedition, which now has no tags and Allen will be reporting it as a loaner that was stolen in a few minutes. That document was notarized days ago and is sitting on his desk back in Huntington. Connie is waiting on his call to turn it over to Calvin. Meanwhile we are going to retrieve a sword and trade it for some cash."

***

My cell rang ten minutes later. "Mr. Kugar? Ruiz here. Are you all right? I understand there was a shooting in San Antonio."

"Yes, Thanks for checking Mr. Ruiz. I am fine. No, it had nothing to do with us. We decided to do some sightseeing before we meet." He must assume we were going to retrieve the sword, but I didn't say it.

"I see," he said, pausing a moment too long as he said it. "And are we still on to see the sword? And am I in any danger?"

"Indeed, we are on, and from what I understand those shootings were probably random violence I suspect. I am just glad we were not there when it happened. The sound of gunfire always makes me uncomfortable. You know how these American cities are these days."

"Yes, I do," he said.

"I will call you back with more details once it is arranged. It will not be in San Antonio."

"Yes, that makes sense. Thank you. I look forward to seeing it with some great anticipation. I will be waiting for your call. By the way, our mutual friend Briscoe Reddix asked to be there too. He said that would give you some reassurance of our legitimacy. Would that be OK with you?"

"No problem, I will enjoy seeing him again. In fact, the only reason I am talking to you is Briscoe's recommendation. I trust him."

"I understand," Ruiz said. "We have always found him trustworthy as well. We have been doing business with him for a long time. Senor Reddix is an old friend."

Chapter 50

We pulled into the yard of a small cabin on a green Arizona mountain with an even smaller outbuilding resembling a springhouse or well house dug back into the ridge. There was a soft wind swaying the pines and the sky was a crisp blue.

"What's this place?" I asked.

"It is my Grandad's secret place. He showed it to me right before he died. He said everyone should have a secret place where they can get away from everyone. He was going to put a bunker here for a survivalist last-ditch place, but he never got around to it. He talked a lot about prepping, but obtaining this remote spot was as far as he got with it.

"The deed was signed over to me and placed in with the sword documents, but it has not been recorded. No one knows I own it, but me."

"And the sword is here?"

"We'll see, won't we?"

I will admit that I am on the paranoid side. That is one of the reasons I'm still walking upright on terra firma. Immediately upon exiting Allen and I both locked and loaded the two AR's. He took the 7.62mm, as he is the better shot. I carried the .223, and we followed Carolyn up to the small building, arms at high port, Allen taking the left, me six meters to his right, scanning the tree line and possible cover for a gunman. There was no movement.

Inside was a small tool room, and a second metal door leading to a storage room with pegboard hung with tools. A yellow Dewalt drill sat on the counter, the battery in the charger glowing red. She took the drill and inserted a

Phillips head driver bit, sat it down on the counter and with a screwdriver and hammer deftly lifted the interior metal door from its loose pin hinges.

"Damn, a woman that is handy with tools too?" She glared at me.

We helped her ease the door down, and she removed the screws holding the top panel of the door, taking off the wood strip. A washer tied to a piece of paracord was glued to the hollow door interior. She pried it loose with a screwdriver and pulled it slow and steady. Soon the end of a thick blue cloth bag appeared. She withdrew the bag, spilling a dozen moisture preventative packets as she did. She untied one end, showing a plain wood scabbard.

"The Honjo Masamune," she said. "Want to compare the temper line with the photos?"

"Considering all the misery this sword has brought since I learned about it, I am not sure I want to touch it." I said.

"No problem," Carolyn said, sliding it back down into the bag and tying the end. "Let me put the door back together and let's get out of here." She was mumbling under her breath about being surprised that someone who dealt in collectibles did not want to touch one of the most collectible items of all time. She was right, I couldn't resist.

I took the cloth bag from her, carefully unwrapped the blade, easing it from its wood scabbard, hefting it, gripping it with two hands, lifting, swaying, reveling in the delicate balance, peering into the glint of the metal and trying to look deeper.

It is said the Samurai's katana is the soul of the Samurai, the badge of their rank, and in the end, their most important possession. This sword was supposed to bring the owner good luck. I hoped that legend was true.

This sword I held was purported to be the best of those swords, and the sword I now gripped in my hands had been the badge of the legendary Samurai warriors that ruled Japan for 400 years. A shogun had worn this sword that decided the fate of nations over those years, in many battles in which defeat meant losing one's head—to a different sharp Samurai sword. How many lives had this one sword changed forever?

One cannot reach out and touch history in a tactile sense, but if open to the vibe I believe an object with history in its core will transmit an indiscernible nuance, a bit of the cosmic universe, an unseen something that penetrates the being, unseen, but you know it is there just the same.

I think that something varies from object to object, from person to person.

What did this sword hold that could transmit to me? What was it saying? I cleared my mind and waited, listening for what it offered. The word came. It wasn't safety, or blood lust, or power. It was something I needed more at this moment. Strength. The sword reeked of strength.

I carefully replaced it in the wood scabbard and protective bag and felt stronger for having touched it. I said nothing to Allen or Carolyn. I did not expect them to understand.

***

We rehung the door, replaced the tools, and placed the sword inside the duffle bag in the back of the van that held the rifles and my shotgun.

For added security that night, the three of us stayed in the same hotel room, a Hampton Inn alongside the interstate that we selected based on nothing more than when we were tired of riding and let our fatigue tell us when to stop.

Allen and I alternated watch. It was not the first time we had swapped watches throughout a night, but it was the cleanest environment in which we had ever done so—with a chair too.

Carolyn slept hard, barely moving. The sword was leaned in the corner behind the door and I cradled my rifle in my arms, a 30-round magazine in, and a sealed plastic cap on a second magazine taped to the first, in reverse position. When the first 30 ran dry, all I had to do was flip the cap off the other side, insert it into the weapon. I could have 30 more rounds in seconds. I had practiced it enough to know.

I also know that in a close firefight I would be lucky to stay alive long enough to get off 60 rounds.

At least the sword part of this would soon be over, I thought.

Chapter 51

Allen went to fetch breakfast, gone so long that I was becoming concerned, but after 45 minutes of anxiety, he was finally back. He gave me a nod that told me he had made the other arrangements I had asked of him while he was out of the room.

I made calls to alert Ruiz, and we wolfed down tasty sausage and egg breakfast burrito's at the restaurant next door before we hit the road. We drove south the next day, through the White Sands Missile range, past Socorro, and mid-afternoon we took a left down a dirt road outside of Las Cruces, toward the Sangre De Christos. Carolyn was puzzled.

"Google Earth," I said. She rolled her eyes. "I was joking. Shooter, one of my buddies from the service, lives near here. On dark Afghanistan nights with nothing but time on our hands, he started talking about Western novels. He read everything Louis L'Amour wrote, and he said L'Amour was known to take a horse and ride the trails, describing the surroundings in his book based on his actual ride.

"Shooter said he and his friends would find an identifiable spot from the book, go there with horses, and ride the same trail, reading the book as they went along.

"The funny thing was he said that if L'Amour said there was a water hole, it would be there, and as L'Amour said, 'and the water will be good to drink.'"

"That sounds like fun," Carolyn said as I told her what Shooter had told me. "It has been years since I've been on a horse. So, you chose this place based on a Louis L'Amour book?"

"No, Shooter recommended this spot," I said.

"Why the story about the L'Amour books then?"

"I like a good story."

"You and your stories," she laughed, "And Ruiz knows to come here?"

"He does now. I sent him the GPS co-ordinates two hours ago. No need to give him time to plan anything."

"Do you trust him?"

"Hell no," I said. "Would you?"

***

We pulled up in a flat open space, several hundred yards from the nearest rise of massive rocks stacked like fallen dominoes behind us. Allen was texting on his phone and I soon saw a plume of dust closing from the direction in which we had come. I watched as a big white Ford Excursion neared. I knew it to be Briscoe. He liked Excursions for their Texas size. When he heard that Ford was going to discontinue them, he had bought three new ones, putting them in storage where he paid someone to keep them maintained so when the one he was driving now wore out he had a replacement. "I figure I have enough of them to last the rest of my life," he told me.

I held up my hand when the vehicle entered the open space, stepping 20 feet in front of the van, and they stopped, maybe 25 yards out. It was close enough. I'm not sure if the hand gesture stopped them or it was the presence of the AR15 cradled in the crook of my arm, but it worked.

"Ever notice how much this place looks like Afghanistan?" Allen said, loud enough for me to hear. "Rock and dirt and nothing else around."

"Don't remind me," I said, "but you are right, right down to our domestic version of the Taliban." His eyes followed mine and quickly he stepped behind the open van door as Ruiz emerged, while Briscoe did the same from the driver side, his son behind him. The reason I had referred to the Taliban was behind Ruiz were two other men, one out far enough from the concealment of the open doors that I could see he carried a Heckler & Koch MP5 submachine gun.

"Keep those guns down or somebody dies, understand?" I said, almost at a shout and certainly in my best command voice. My rifle had gone to my shoulder by instinct the moment I saw his firearm, although I knew I was exposed.

I didn't have to ask if Allen had his rifle at the ready, we had endured the same training. My left flank was secure. I had lost track of Carolyn, but I heard her feet rustle a few feet behind me.

"You have the cash?" I asked Ruiz.

"Well we have had a complication with that," he said. "It will be here in a minute. Do you have the sword?" I refused to answer.

That was when I heard the chopper, coming in low and from the back side of the hill, popping up over the small rise and then down close to the ground, circling the rocks on the rise twice, slow, and making two rounds around us, kicking up a lot of dust and blinding us from Ruiz and his group.

I turned back to the van, pushing Carolyn ahead of me. I don't know how he did it, but in the confusion, noise, and cloud of dust, one of the men with Ruiz appeared out of the dust, between us and the van. He was raising his MP5 when I shoved the stock of my AR into the lower side of his jaw. He went down hard, and I kicked the MP5 under the van. He didn't move, out cold or dead. I didn't care which. If he moved, I would make it the latter quick enough.

"Stay down," I warned. I do not know if he heard me, but he did not move.

As the dust settled Allen snickered. Ruiz and Briscoe both had drawn handguns, extending them between the door and frame of the Excursion on each side.

The other man with the MP5 had it leveled. I couldn't see what Damon was carrying, but I was aware I was dealing with someone experienced with firearms, a cop. He was not in uniform. I knew he would have his hand on a firearm, probably down at his side or behind his back. He was concealed by the door.

The chopper settled to the ground on our front left, half distance between our van and Briscoe's Excursion.

I was behind one open door of the van; Allen was behind the other, our rifles in the space between the door and the frame.

"What do you think is so funny?"

"A real Mexican standoff, compadre." Allen said. "Just like in the movies."

"Yeah, and long odds, seven against three."

"Two of the three are Marines," Allen said. "So that makes it about even."

Chapter 52

The door of the chopper opened, and Thomas McMasters emerged, a white bandage taped on his forehead, along with another man also carrying an MP5 and another Hispanic man in a spotless light brown suit empty-handed. He was not sweating in the suit, despite the heat.

"Manuel Azeveda," I heard Carolyn say under her breath. McMasters was confident in his numbers, thinking he had pulled off a coup. He didn't speak but I knew what was coming, he had it written all over his smug face. I waited until he had his pistol halfway out of his belt before I shot him three times, neck and head. He collapsed.

To their credit the others did not start shooting—they were in control of themselves.

"Anyone else cares to dance?" I said.

"Why did you do that?" Ruiz screamed.

"He was drawing, I warned him already. I'm warning you now," I said.

"Now, Now, Mr. Kugar," Azeveda said, stepping forward. "We do not want more gunplay; we only want a sword. Whatever problem you had with Thomas; you have just settled. I mean you no harm. No need for any more violence. I understand Thomas had uh, let's say an unnatural desire for the sword, but," he looked down at the bleeding body, "It appears we have resolved his problem. I have no problem with you, sir."

Azeveda nodded to Ruiz and the others, and they lowered their firearms. I didn't.

"Thomas was the one that wanted everything, and everyone eliminated," Azeveda said. "I have a different option. I desire the sword; The Japanese with who I do business can wield much political power in exchange for that sword."

"Not power, corruption, you mean."

"Tomato, To-mah-toe," he smiled a bright bleached tooth smile. It was a vicious smile. I kept my cheek on the rifle.

"And for that, we get how much?" I asked.

"How much are your lives worth?" Azeveda said, his voice turning icy and stern. "I'm offering that." Ruiz, his gunman, Briscoe, and his son had all moved completely behind the Excursion's open doors, out of a direct line of fire. I felt the tenseness of the moment escalating.

"Allen?"

"I got 'em."

"I don't think so, Senor Azeveda, nothing personal but I do not believe you," I said.

"Ah, so you know my name," Azeveda said, "There is someone here who can attest to my word, isn't there Carolyn," he said. "Ask her," Carolyn said nothing.

"OK, the cat has her tongue, so I will explain. When Thomas gave her to me, I told her that when I was tired of her that I would let her go and not bother her. I didn't force her to work in one of my houses, despite what a young pretty Anglo would bring there. I gave up a lot of money because I honored what I promised her when we started. I keep my word, do I not Carolyn?"

"Carolyn?" I said. Still, no answer but I heard a sob behind me. "Say something."

Azeveda recognized something in my tone. "Oh, I'm sure you have enjoyed her favors, haven't you? I trained her well in how to please a man." He laughed. The rifle barrel shook, revealing my shaking hands. I almost shot him then.

"Has she told you about herself? How she stole away from her Grandfather to rejoin Thomas when he thought she was going on a senior trip but instead came to me? She is a wild one. She said she loved me. Has she said that to you? She's such a pretty liar." I fought to keep my finger along the frame of the rifle and away from the trigger.

"Do you know she worked in one of my houses for a week, for the experience, to prove to me she was willing. Even after I told her I wouldn't force her. Who was I to stop a pretty Anglo being a *puta*? Tell him it's true, Carolyn. Tell him how you whored for me."

"It's true," I heard her say. "I'm sorry, Max, It's true."

"I kept my word. I didn't kill her Grandfather, because I promised her I would not since she was so nice to me."

"You get the sword, you leave, that's it? We hear nothing more from you?" I said. I didn't want to hear any more about Carolyn. I dropped my finger to the trigger guard, closer to the trigger.

"That's true, my word."

"Have your man come closer, unarmed," I said. Azeveda's bodyguard dropped his firearm and trotted toward us. I changed my aim to him. "Give it to him, Carolyn." She reached into the van for the long blue cloth bag. At six feet from the approaching man, she tossed it on the ground. "Back away Carolyn," I said. She did and the man stepped forward. He picked up the sword from the dirt and dog trotted back to the chopper.

Azeveda smiled. "OK, Carolyn. Now is the time," he said. I heard a click, the distinct sound of a hammer being cocked, and turned to see her holding the .38 on me, my own pistol in a trembling hand. It takes a hefty pull to fire a J-frame Smith & Wesson double action, close to a nine-pound trigger pull. Cock it to fire single action, as Carolyn had done, with the way I honed the action on my

pistols, the trigger pull was closer to three or four pounds—
touch it and breathe hard and it would fire. She had her
finger on the trigger and it was pointed at my head. I could
see the hollow point expansion rounds in the cylinder.

"I've kept up my end, Carolyn," Azeveda said.
"Your brother is dead and not by my hand. You can take out
the man who killed him."

I was facing Carolyn. Out of the corner of my eye, I
saw the bodyguard put the sword inside the chopper.

"OK, kill him and let's go, Carolyn." Azeveda said.
"Remember how you were trained to do as I say. Do it. We
have other things to do today."

"No, Carolyn," I said.

"I warned you to not get emotional," she said. "No
way you would want me after what he's told you. And all of
it is true. No one would want me. I've always known it."

"That's the past. What about the future? Mrs.
Madison." I saw the words hit, her back straightened. "I see
the woman you are now. Put that gun down." I didn't know
where this was ending, but there was one thing I had to get
out. "I love you, Carolyn."

"Oh fuck," Allen said softly. "Here we go again.
He's in love with another fucking Carolyn."

Carolyn said, "You are fucking crazy."

"Agreed," Allen said without taking his face from
the rifle covering the others.

"Yes, no argument. Put the fucking gun down and
let's get this deal finalized."

"Mean it?" she asked. "You love me?"

"Truthful and serious. You know I wouldn't lie
about something like that. I've fought it as long as I can-- I
love you. Despite that wall you have up, I've seen you let it
down. You can still love too if you let yourself."

I saw her wavering, but as they say about your life flashing before your eyes, I saw it, nothing but a long line of Carolyns, the hurt, the pain, the sadness. Now here I was again—with a Carolyn. Maybe it was time to stop all the bullshit.

"Put it down or pull the trigger. I'm fine with it either way; I've done the best I could." I said. She trembled and for a moment I swear I thought she was going to shoot. I braced for it; the flash followed by the blackness. My body tensed. She lowered the pistol.

I don't know what Azeveda meant by starting the chopper, or if he was tired of waiting for Carolyn to act, but what followed made whatever he was thinking by doing that a moot point. The chopper started to lift, stirring dust, blinding everyone. The dust began to settle as the chopper lifted away. Azeveda was still there, but behind the back of the Excursion with the others. His bodyguard was holding his MP5 again. The man I had slugged with the rifle had scurried back behind the Excursion as well. Long odds.

"Sorry it must end this way, Carolyn, you know you are mine and you had the chance to leave, loco Gringa" Azeveda said, louder. "I promised you could all go, but Mr. Ruiz and Reddix did not. I had to be sure you had the sword first."

"Your word…"

"Oh yes, my word is worthless, this is business," he said.

"Briscoe," I said. "I never figured you."

"Sorry Max, my boy has been dealing with Azeveda for years."

"He's a cop," I said.

"He was, in Del Rio. Funny how that started. One day an ugly old Mexican man came up to him and said he wanted Damon here to guard a drug shipment that was crossing the river that night. You've known Damon since he was little, he's a good boy. Damon said he wouldn't do it.

"The man handed him a photo album of Damon, his wife, his kids—my grandkids, dammit, not to mention me and my wife. They threatened all of us. The old man said if Damon didn't guard the shipment, that everyone in that photo album would be dead within two days. Damon's a good boy, but a practical one.

"You know me, Max, always looking to make a deal. If you can't beat'em is how the saying goes. Through Damon, once I got inside the contacts, I started making some deals. No need to threaten us, better that we are partners on several things. I have to stand with my partners."

"Dying for them part of that loyalty?" I asked.

"Well, you know how it is," Briscoe said with a smug smile. His shoulder shrug that told me he had a different idea on how this was going to end than I did.

"Enough talk," Ruiz said, "Let's get this over with."

"Wait," I said. It was enough to make them pause for a second or two, their minds instinctively reacting to the voiced command, that moment of hesitation to determine who said it, should the command be obeyed, flashing through the brain in fractions of a second, but a delay just the same.

I had raised my hand high as I spoke. They might have thought it a surrender gesture, but I flattened my hand at the wrist, my index finger extended, I pointed to Ruiz. I counted. "One. Two." On the count of three was when Ruiz's head exploded. The sound of the shot reached our ears a second later. Ruiz was already dead.

Allen was on ready, code red, and as Ruiz fell against the door Allen began firing. He took down the two bodyguards with professional quick double taps to each, firing through the windows of the Excursion, more by feel than by visibility, because the glass spiderwebbed with the first shot. An M4 would have been a burst of three shots but two shots each from a .308 as fast as Allen could pull the trigger still did the job.

I fired four rounds at Briscoe through the car door. I stack my magazines with an armor piercing round, soft nose, AP, soft nose, AP in the magazine just in case I run into body armor, and I wasn't sure if it would penetrate the door panel. I didn't wait to see. I moved my point of aim and shot his ankles out from under him. He collapsed behind the door for two more rounds to his chest.

Damon was quick, and in the melee, I lost track of him. Now he was coming up almost behind me, on my left side. With my rifle nested in the gap of the door, there was no way I could move the rifle around in time to take him. His mistake was he had not kept his pistol on me when he approached, lowering it to step over a deep wash. His firearm was down when he crossed the wash to get closer.

My pistol was holstered. This is not good, I thought.

If Damon's pistol had been holstered, he was within a range that I stood a chance to rush him with a knife and get to him before he could draw and fire. Thirty-two feet is the maximum range and still no guarantee of it working.

Damon was closer than that. But his pistol was not holstered, and his police training would have taught him to backpedal away from my rush, giving him plenty of time to raise his pistol and fire.

I was calm, amazingly calm. Maybe this time I am dead, I thought. So, close those other times in Afghanistan to end it here? It is not like we can choose. Our maker does the choosing of the time and the place.

Chapter 53

In my teenage years on the road to Atlanta, south of Blairsville, Georgia, a gun collector had briefly opened a museum entitled "Guns of the Gunfighters." Inside his makeshift museum, he had utilized old car windshields as the panes for his displays and boasted a nice collection of Single Action Army Colt Peacemakers and related firearms, including a few nice vintage Henry rifles.

What I remembered most about that visit was that he was a competitive quickdraw shooter. They had perfected the competition to the point that the shooter's holsters were metal lined, and the drawing of a pistol tripped a timer, with the timing ending when the target was hit.

My Dad and I showed more interest than most tourists that stopped by that day, and he offered a demonstration of his quick draw.

He had his teenage daughter don a thick leather fringed jacket, thick gloves, and walk off 15 paces, holding two balloons, one in each hand, with her back to us. He lined up sideways to her, and in a flash, more like a whip-bang, he had burst both balloons with his daughter unhurt, obviously firing rat shot in his cartridges.

He explained that the trick was one did not need to raise the pistol up to shoulder level. Clear leather a half inch from the holster, tilt the barrel level with your belt, your hand no higher than your buckle, and fire from the waist. He carried his pistol in a crossdraw holster.

"You turn your body sideways because that makes a smaller target. Remember, all you must do is clear leather and shoot. The faster shot always wins. At pistol range for a gunfight, there is no need to aim or move it more than an inch from the holster. Rely on your instinct," the fast draw expert explained.

That one day in a North Georgia tourist trap was why I carry my pistol in a cross-draw holster on my left side, like Doc Holliday in the Tombstone movie. He shoots from the waist in the scene he kills Johnny Ringo.

I couldn't swing my rifle as Damon approached, but my hand was already at my waist, pulling my Glock from the holster, raising the barrel so fast it brushed the edge of the holster and firing from my waist position, the double-tap two round burst was training and reflex. I saw a puff of dust from his chest as each round struck.

Damon never raised his pistol from his side and tumbled back into the wash.

***

I had lost track of Azevada. Azevada was game, I will give him that.

In the excitement from the rear of the Excursion, he had flanked us and had come up behind me, unseen. His voice was the first indication he was behind me. It was impossible to turn in time. "Now you..." he started to say but couldn't finish, his words turning into a gasp that turned into a red gurgle filling his mouth, running down his cheek. I heard three quick pops and he pitched forward into the desert dust without moving. Three red spots in a triangle were spreading spots of red in his mid-back, one round between his shoulder blades, the other two lower.

It was over that quick.

Three life-destroying seconds. Carolyn was behind him, maybe five feet away in a double hand stance, just like I had shown her. She was still pointing the pistol at

Azeveda's prone body. I didn't speak, and she fired the other two rounds into his corpse. She froze in that stance, and I stepped to her and gently removed the empty pistol from her shaking hands, leading her to the van and helping her inside where she put her face in her hands, her shoulder shivering.

There was a silence over the scene, the only sounds our heavy breathing.

I heard the "whump" and the thud of Damon's body falling before I heard the crack of the rifle. Damon had struggled to his feet and from the wash was trying to raise a Beretta pistol. I had forgotten that as a cop he would be wearing body armor. That lapse almost cost me my life.

The round that took out Damon was a neck shot near the chest. That was when I realized the blood dripping down my arm from a graze. "You OK?" I asked Allen.

"Affirmative," he said, sitting down in the sand, his rifle in his lap. By instinct, he was already changing to a fresh magazine. The adrenaline was fading. "Shit, I'm getting too old for this shit," Allen said.

"Carolyn?" She didn't speak for a minute and looked up at me, tears streaking her dusty face.

"You son-of-a-bitch. You gave away the sword. I need that money. Now, what am I going to do?" She burst into sobs. The stress of the moment was overwhelming. That happens when death comes to look you in the eye and you realize that the tiniest bit of a second, the measure of a thousandth of an inch, is often the only reason you are alive, and the other person is dead.

And there is another reaction too, a Marine response, when you look into those empty dark eyes of the reaper and can scream, "fuck you – not today."

"I glanced over at Allen as he scowled at Carolyn. "Not a word."

"A Carolyn, what did you expect? You know better," he said.

"Guess some people never learn," I said.

"Some dumbasses never learn, and they are always dumbasses," Allen said.

"Love you too," I said.

Carolyn got out and stomped to the back of the van, still crying, arms crossed looking out at the mountains behind her, overwhelmed with the shock of death so close. Her outburst was a stress release. She was alive, but I wasn't sure she had comprehended that yet.

Carolyn caught a glint of light from the rocks in the far hill, and I think it was then she figured out one of the reasons we were all still upright and breathing.

"Who shot the cop?" she asked. "And Ruiz? At first, I thought Azevada might have shot Ruiz from behind, but he had no reason."

"Shooter, a brother of ours in the rocks," I said. "They didn't see him from the chopper when they circled. We learned how to cover in place a long time ago. Ruiz thought we were out of range even if someone had managed to hide. He did not understand the magic of the .338 Lapua. It has a range of over a mile with an experienced hand. Shooter is one of the best shots I've ever known. Snipered with Allen in the Helmund. Has 72 confirmed kills. He lives in Las Cruces now. We gave him a call for security, and he was willing to help."

***

"Money that important to you?" I asked her later, "Are you pissed about losing the sword?"

"Money is all I've ever been able to count on," she said. "I tried to love with Manuel as a teenager and it burned me out. I was too young. I learned after that. I'm cold. I can't love. Too much to lose by loving."

"So, what he said was true?"

"I told you it was. I was in love, I knew he was tired of me; I wanted to prove to him I was as good as any of his other girls, so I went into one of his brothels for a week. No one there knew I was his girlfriend," she said. "While I was working there, I came to my senses. I wanted to get away—and that was when he decided he wanted to keep me, but he did keep his word." She looked up at me with a sorrowful expression, her eyes wet. "I warned you not to get emotional with me. I was young and stupid."

"We all are at that age. But you are not as cold as you claim. You let the emotion in when you were holding that gun on me. You didn't shoot," I said.

"Don't get on your high horse, I definitely thought about it."

"I knew you wouldn't," I said.

"And what made you so sure?"

"Because when we were shooting in North Carolina and went over the protocol again at the beach. You know when you raise the gun it is time to fire, no hesitation. You didn't fire."

"You certain about that?" she said. "Maybe I wasn't paying as much attention to your instructions as you thought." I ignored her comment.

"That's why I told you I loved you."

"Huh?"

"That's when I knew you loved me too. You hesitated. You didn't shoot."

Carolyn looked at me and her face softened. "No one has told me they loved me in forever. You sounded like you meant it. I don't know if I've ever heard those words said to me in that way."

"I'm not good at lying, so I generally mean what I say."

"Generally?"

I glanced over at Allen who was raising his eyebrows and mouthing the word, "Carolyn."

"We need to talk about this another time; we don't need to be here when these bodies are discovered," I said. Carolyn was content to leave it at that, but it was a conversation we must have.

Chapter 54

"Everything clear?" I asked Allen.

"Clear enough." He dialed his cell. "Shooter? Anything coming our way, dust? Anything?" Allen looked up at me. "We're good." Then into the phone, he told Shooter, "Catch up with us in El Paso. Fine. Let's get the hell out of here before we must explain all these dead bodies. Thanks, brother." As we drove away, I looked in the back seat of the van.

Carolyn had zoned out. She lay with her head back in the corner with her eyes closed.

Allen looked back over his shoulder. "Carolyn," was all he said, grinning.

"I know." I answered.

***

"We need to ditch the van," I said.

"Don't worry," Allen said, "I have a plan."

A few hours later Allen dropped Carolyn and I at a Holiday Inn Express off I-10, all our gear in gun cases, large canvas bags, and a couple of suitcases in a pile at the foot of the bed.

"Where did Allen go?" Carolyn asked as she came out from the shower draped in a towel.

"To get rid of the van."

"How does he propose to do that? Something as big as a van is kinda hard to hide, isn't it?

"He's going down to a Latino bar area near the bridge into Mexico," I said. "Allen will leave the door unlocked, the window rolled down, and the keys in the van. It will be in Mexico by dark. Shooter is picking him up at the bar and bringing him back here."

Shooter and Allen returned in less than an hour. Shooter came into the room with a big smile.

"Damn that's the prettiest black face I've seen in a year," I said, pulling him in for a hug.

"You white boys are all the same, black is beautiful," he joked. "Good to see you, man."

"I owe you big for the backup," I said. "Thank you, more than you know."

"Oh, I know," Shooter said. "Damned if it wasn't shaping up into one of those damn Custer things you white boys always seem to be getting your asses into. Lucky for you I was there to save your ass."

"Wasn't the first time," I smiled.

"And probably not the last," Shooter said. "And indeed, you do owe me, and I plan to cash it in sometimes this summer," he said. "Maria and the rug rats want a vacation and I could use some native trout fishing."

"I'll get you into spots no stocked rainbow has ever seen," I said.

"Promises, promises," Shooter said to Allen.

"Nah, he doesn't joke about trout fishing," Allen said. "Much too serious a subject for joking."

"I'll plan on seeing you in the summer then brother," I said.

"I'm going to surprise you and show up," he promised.

"I'm counting on it," I promised him the loan of a cabin on the lake and all the booze on me.

Carolyn was dressed by then, emerging from the bathroom, jean shorts, a tank top, and a real smile that melts hearts.

I introduced them. "Shooter, Carolyn. Carolyn, Shooter."

"Damn," Shooter said, dragging the word out over a few seconds as he looked her up and down, "You are lovely, girl." Shooter said. "Nice to meet you." Shooter straightened, a shocked glance over at Allen. "I hear the boy, right? Did he say, Carolyn?"

"Indeed, he did brother," Allen said.

Shooter said nothing more, standing there shaking his head back and forth, looking down at the floor with a silly smile. Finally, he looked up, glancing back and forth between Allen and I. "No words," he said.

"Good," I said. Carolyn looked confused but didn't say anything.

"Wish I could stay, but I gotta pick up a kid at pre-school," Shooter said. "Gotta run." We shook hands again, another hug, he hugged Carolyn too, smiled and said, "Damn, that's was pretty good. One more for the road girl," and he pulled her tight again.

"Nice, much too nice for a white boy like you," he said, smiling at me. "Carolyn," he said with no further comment other than a snickered "HeHeHe" and shaking his head. He added, "Semper Fi," as he went out the door.

"Shooter seemed like a nice man," Carolyn said.

"I thought you said you were good at reading people," I said.

"Oh, he's nice if you are on his side. Not so much if you are a Taliban taking pot-shots at Marines. They had a bounty on his head."

"Really?"

"Yeah, but they didn't call him "Shooter", they had another name for him, I said. "He was known to them as 'The Black Death.'"

Chapter 55

I needed to feel the safety of my mountains. It was too dry, flat, and rocky where we were, and home was a world away from where all the pursuit had ended, and I wanted to sure there was no one else on our trail. A world away from all this was where I wanted to be, and I was headed that way at 75 miles per hour.

Allen made a nice deal with an online auction and landed a 10-year old Benz that we picked up at the auction's facility in El Paso. I dropped him off at the airport. I figured we would have trouble getting by TSA with the fake ID's we still carried, so flying was not in the cards for us.

We decided to return out I-20. I expected Carolyn to bolt and go back to Santa Barbara when I let Allen out at the airport, but she didn't, remaining in the car as if we were still on the run. I was tired of being unsure though.

"Do you want to go back with me?" I asked.

"I'll ride back with you for the company," she said. "You've talked too much about how you hate to travel alone." I didn't remember telling her that, but I probably did. "Besides," she said. "I need to say goodbye to Street. I would buy him from you know."

"Even had we sold that sword for 20 million it was not enough to buy my dog," I said. I was glad she was staying close because I had a surprise she wasn't expecting; I was only waiting for the right moment to spring it. I wouldn't know until later that she had a surprise of her own.

Carolyn lowered the seat, pulled a jacket over her and dozed for the first 200 miles, stirring, mumbling in her sleep at times, restless. She woke when I pulled into a Scholtzsky's.

"We don't have these at home anymore. I miss that giant sandwich. Wanna go in?" I said.

I saw the realization hit her, there was no one chasing us now, no reason for anyone to harm us, save for revenge for some of the bodies we left in the New Mexico desert and that was not likely.

The police would not be too interested in solving those once they got into the backgrounds of the dead. The cartel people would step someone up into Azevada's spot— standard course of business. With the chopper pilot being able to take them straight to the shootout location, I expected there would be some quick shallow graves and a white Excursion making its way to Mexico within a day. There was no need for burials or funerals to make waves with the police and politicians in that part of the world. There was no point that needed to be made to a rival group, so silence was best.

Back on the road, my windshield time was giving me time to rewind, replay, reanalyze. "Carolyn, Avezeda said after I shot your brother that he had done as he promised."

"Yes."

"I don't understand."

"I thought I loved Manuel, but after my Grandfather braced him, he threatened to kill Grandad. I stayed to protect Grandad, but I never stopped hating my brother for giving me to Manuel. My own brother gave me away to a stranger for business reasons, his own sister. When I left Manuel, I told him I would not come back until he was no longer doing business with my brother, when my brother was dead. He offered to kill Thomas. I told him no, he was still my brother, and there was no way I could be with him knowing he had a hand in killing my brother in order to be with me, or hurt my Grandfather who was the only father I ever knew.

"Manuel wanted me back. He contacted me again after he learned my Grandfather had died. But there was still Thomas and I was steadfast. And I have grown up. I'm not a 16-year-old impressionable girl anymore."

"What about you?" I asked.

"What about me?"

"Did you want him back?"

"You are still alive, aren't you?" Carolyn said. "If I had wanted him, I would have pulled that trigger on you, not him, back there in the desert. Your body would be there, and I would be at a lavish hacienda in Mexico right now."

"I killed your brother," I said.

"Yes. But not over your being with me. He was evil. I know that. He needed killing; I am old enough to understand that now. I should have let Manuel kill him years ago and there wouldn't be so many people dead today."

"I might not have met you then," I said.

"You really don't know if that is a good thing or a bad thing yet though, do you?" she said with a wry smile.

Chapter 56

I was driving through the high desert and it was closing dark, enough to make out the features but still dark enough that headlights were on, driving through a rocky pass. I could see 50 miles of a headlight-lit snaking road twisting around two well-lit towns, identified by the red Conoco signs sticking up like little flags on a cake. It was beautiful. But the view did not have my green and blue mountains in it. I was getting homesick. My cell buzzed and I answered.

"Really," I said to my cousin, the one who was working at the U. S. Embassy in Japan. "You sure?" He continued talking for several minutes. "OK, I will get back with you, thanks."

"What was that?" Carolyn asked.

"My cousin in Japan. I had asked him to check on a few things."

"Like what?"

"Let me ask you something," I said without answering her question. "If your brother is dead, are there any other heirs in your family."

"No. He had no wife, no kids."

"So you would inherit his interest in the Japanese electric car business?"

"I never thought of that," she said, "but maybe." She thought for a minute and then exploded. "You son-of-a-bitch, are you implying that I did anything different from what I told you?"

"Have you?"

Carolyn looked at me. "Azeveda told you everything I've held back. You know everything there is to know about me. If not, ask and I will tell you now. I'm hiding anything from you."

"Did you consider you might inherit his stock in the Japanese company if anything ever happened to him?"

"Hell no. I don't give a shit about a battery powered car."

"It might be a lot of money. A fortune. You told me back in the desert that the only thing you've learned you could rely on is money."

"Maybe I've changed my view on part of that," she said. "Money is nice, but I don't want anything to come to me because of what happened back there in the desert. That's blood money. Karma will come around someday."

"Even if they started it and brought it on themselves."

"Even then." Carolyn wasn't smiling or acting. "This ordeal has changed me. There's more to life than money."

"Such as?"

"Tell me you love me again, just like you did in the desert. If you meant it."

I half turned in the seat, slowing down and looking her straight in the face. "I meant it. I love you Carolyn McMasters."

Carolyn paused, taking deeper breaths, struggling. Her eyes teared. I saw vulnerability in her face that remained instead of the brief flashes before. She was open for the first time since I had met her. "What if I love you too?"

"Then Hallelujah. Do you?"

"I don't know. I don't know how that is supposed to feel anymore," she said.

"Then you don't." I said. "If you did you would know it without a doubt." It was not the best answer, but it was the truth. Even as I said it, I felt her features harden again and she turned her back to me looking out at the high desert, the soft hum of the tires on the hot pavement singing a lullaby that soon had her reclined back in her seat asleep.

I continued driving late into a disappointing night, so late that once we got the room, sleep was the only thing on my mind. I had more to say to her, but I felt it better said in the light of day after a good night's sleep.

Chapter 57

The next morning Carolyn looked at me with swollen red eyes. "Are you OK?"

"No. I didn't sleep much."

"Why not?"

"There's something I haven't told you. It's big, I'm afraid. It is bad," Carolyn said.

"Tell me."

"I'm afraid to. I'm afraid you'll be mad at me for not telling you before, I'm afraid it will be more than you can..." Carolyn bawled, "I'm afraid you won't love me anymore after I've just now discovered you love me."

"Try me. The only way to know," I said.

Carolyn tried to regain her composure and after a few sips of water straightened. "You know when I was working in Austin?"

"Stripping?"

"Yes."

"There's more to it."

"OK."

"I wasn't a 16-year-old being taken advantage of in Mexico. I chose to do it again as an adult, 21-years-old."

"What?"

"I was an escort for a couple of months. Several of the girls were."

"The strip club customers?" I asked.

"Hell no, even escorts have better sense than to date strip club customers, how would you get them to come in and spend hundreds of dollars a couple of times a month if they could fuck you for less? Besides the police watch the clubs and the managers would be on your ass too."

"You were a hooker? How long?" I asked.

"Couple of months," she stopped. "OK, three months, mostly weekends. I stopped when I got the bit part in the movie and left Texas."

"OK." I said. "And since?"

"Nothing since. I was determined I would be different in California. I had a new start."

"OK," I repeated.

"OK what?" she asked. "You do not seem upset. Can you love a woman who was a whore?"

"I determined that back in the desert. So yeah, looks like I do," I said. "I'm not worried about your past; I'm worried about your future—with me, if you can be sure that you love me."

There it was again, the 900-pound gorilla, and she still sat mute, staring out the window away from me, still not giving a concrete answer.

We slept together that night, but it was not a hot burning passion like the days before, it was as if a sadness came with it, like neither of us were going to like the way this ended, but we clung to each other just the same, a long inevitable goodbye.

Chapter 58

Allen called the morning of the third day of our return trip to check on us. "Things going OK?"

"They are," I said. "You take enough from the Madison account to cover your out of pocket?" I asked.

"Hell no. Cars are expensive, especially when you buy one and give one away to some El Paso car thief."

"I need you to do something. No questions," I said. As he listened on his cell, he followed my directions to the spot under the oak behind his shop. "Dig down," I said.

"What the fuck?" He found the stash.

"It's yours," I said. "Offsetting expenses. I'll get even with you as soon as I can."

"This is your cash and coins?" Allen asked. "I'll hold it till you get here."

"Not mine brother, you found buried on your land with no one laying claim to it. It's yours. Legally."

"You don't have to do that," he said. "That's not why I helped."

"No, I don't have to, but I want to."

"OK brother, I've tried to be nice and give it back three times. Now I'm gonna keep it, Godfather."

"Good", I laughed. "Why'd you call me godfather?"

"Cause when the baby gets here that is how you really pay me back for the help. You are gonna be an uncle, of sorts."

"Connie is preggers?"

"That's what the doctor said. Good thing I didn't know before I left. You might have been going solo on your little adventure."

"I know you better than that," I said. "But thanks."

"Always. Semper Fi."

"Semper Fi, brother."

***

"I'll be damned," I said as I ended the call.

"What?"

"Allen's going to be a daddy. He wants me to be the godfather. That's an honor."

"Sure is. Big responsibility. Are you up to it?" Carolyn asked.

"I have to be. It's not like it is a choice." I was smiling.

***

We stopped for gas at a large truck stop with a travel store, and there was a Walgreens across the street. "You have any ibuprofen with you?" Carolyn asked.

"No."

"I need to run over there for a minute while you get the gas," she said. "I'm not paying convenience store prices for a pain killer when I can walk 50 steps." She was back before I finished paying for the gas. With the fresh coffee from the truck stop, she opened the bottle and washed three pain killers down, replacing the bottle into the Walgreens bag and cramming it into her cavernous purse.

Back on the road with the silence and boredom setting in, I thought it was time to bring up something I had been dreading. "There's something else I need to talk to you about," I said. "Last night it didn't seem right. You said you had no interest in your brother's deal on the battery cars."

"That's right."

"Good. I have bad news about that. My cousin had the company checked out. It's a scam. Going to hit the papers in Japan any day now. Arrests have already been made over there."

"So, all the money my brother gave them, all this crap about the sword..."

"Yep, for nothing."

"In a way, it sums up his life," she said. "I guess it is best that that damn sword is gone too, for all the trouble it caused. I wonder what they did with it in Mexico. They can't use it to curry favor with the Japanese now, can they?"

"I'd say that sword we gave them is probably hanging on some drug dealer's wall, along with a long story that will impress everyone he tells it to. I don't think the Japanese in the end would be interested in the sword anyway."

"I have no stock in a company, no priceless sword, too old for an acting career, too old to strip, my house will be foreclosed on in another month or two. I guess I can use what money I have left for a plane ticket back to Santa Barbara and see if I can find a waitress job. The public assistance thing is pretty good there."

"You dwell on this age thing too much," I said. "Lot of sugar daddies would like to have you around. Hell, a lot of men would love to have you around." She knew I was joking and played along.

"I know, for a while, but even sugar daddies eventually start wanting someone younger."

"What about staying in the mountains—with me."

"Hell, I checked you out, remember? You barely get by on what you make."

"So, I can't afford you? I know you'd be high maintenance."

"I am, but I could probably make an exception in special circumstances. I suspect in the future that I'm not going to be as high maintenance as I once was."

"Two can live as cheaply as one if you pay attention to the pennies," I said.

"You're serious?"

"Yes, but only if you love me." The silence threatened to end the conversation—as it had previously—confirming and continuing my lack of luck with Carolyns.

"I've been thinking about that, most of the night actually. The different sides of my brain fought all night long, the practical and emotional."

"And how did that turn out. Who won?"

"Both actually. They came to the same conclusion, both practical and emotional."

"And what was that?" I asked.

"I love you," Carolyn said with a tremble in her voice. "And I know it. No doubt. Look at me, I'm shaking. Yes, I love you." She threw her arms around me and nearly wrecked us, her movement causing me to swerve into the empty left lane. I got the car back under control and laughed. She was tearing up. "Shit I can't believe I'm acting like this."

"I love you too," I said. I'm not sure that I didn't have a tear or two also.

"I know." She snuggled over the console and under my arm. "Hold me," she said, and we rode like that for an hour, until she moved away. "That damn console is bruising my rib," she laughed.

I was stunned at the turn of events. My life looked like it was changing. For the better, with a Carolyn. But then the phone rang.

Chapter 59

I do not like Journey. Yeah, I know Steve Perry has the voice, and the bass player was on American Idol, but their music does not move me. But today, for some reason when I turned on the radio "Don't Stop Believin'" was on Sirius. The volume was up too loud, and the lyrics that stuck before I could turn down the volume was "…roll the dice, just one more time."

Those words pounded inside my head, like a force I could not stop, defying all caution or reason. The phone call had altered some of my thinking—and the song from a group I did not care for did the rest.

"We have to make a side trip," I said.

"Where?"

"New Orleans."

"I've always wanted to go to New Orleans," Carolyn said. "I almost went to Mardi Gras once. A bunch of girls from the club were going when I was in Austin. They came back with a lot of beads. Flashing boobs is not a stretch for a girl who spends most of her nights topless." Then she paused. "Why are we going to New Orleans?" Carolyn studied my face. "OK, you're not a good liar like you said. And you know I can read you. You're holding out on me."

"Yeah, I am," I said, unable to resist smiling. "Before we get in further, I must ask you something, but I don't have the proper hardware for it. I'm tired of putting it off when my mind is made up about what I should do."

"OK."

"Will you marry me?"

"What?"

"Do I have to repeat it?"

"No, I heard you. I don't believe I heard you, but I heard you. You just asked me to marry you. But yeah, I want to hear you say it again."

"I did say it, and I will say it again. Will? You? Marry? Me?" I said.

"After all you know about me. You want to risk that? You know how the hard parts of my life have nearly destroyed me and you still want me? Used goods? Well used goods? You know you don't have to marry me. I'm not sure I'm the good little wife kind. I'll live with you. A piece of paper is not that big a thing these days."

"Yes. I know about you and your past. I know that if I asked, you will move in with me. That wasn't the question. Will you marry me? Don't make me ask again."

Carolyn was hyperventilating, gasping for breath before gushing, "Yes, Yes, oh hell yes!"

"Don't try to wreck us again," I said, bracing at the wheel.

"I won't, I'll be good. When?" she said.

"Whenever you want."

"You don't want to live together a while just to be sure?" Carolyn asked.

"I'm sure. But we will wait if you want to."

"No, I don't want to wait," she said.

"When we get home then, so we can invite some friends?" I said. "You have friends you would like to be there?"

"Only a couple. It costs a lot to fly cross country you know."

"What if money was no object?"

"Even then, maybe four friends total," she said.

"Call 'em."

"Where are we going to get the money?" she asked.

"It's we now, huh?"

"Damn right buster, you made the offer and I accepted. That is a binding contract. We are a 'we' from this moment forward." I liked the sound of that.

"Then I must make a confession to my fiancée, everything up front, nothing held back from here on. Agreed?"

"I thought we've already done that." She caught my scowl. "OK, agreed. Unless it is something I forgot, and I will tell you if I remember something I haven't told you," she said. "But all the big things I've confessed. You know all about me now. But be honest, you first."

"Allen went to an upscale gun collectors store in Atlanta on his way out to join us and bought a nice samurai sword in a wooden scabbard. A nice five grand sword, no more than that."

"OK."

"He swapped it out for the Honjo Masamune and put the cheaper sword into the blue cloth case that had stored the original. The sword he bought in Atlanta was the sword they took in the chopper. It's a nice sword and no one will know for sure until they start comparing the hamon line. I doubt the new owners know enough about swords to do that."

"Oh shit." She said. "You still have the Honjo?"

"It's in the trunk."

"Pull over now, I want to throw the damn thing in the swamp. It's bad luck. We do not need to start our life together with bad luck."

"No, it's not, never was bad luck," I said. "It is the Muramasa swords that bring bad luck to their owners. It is common knowledge in Japan. The owners of the Honjo ruled Japan for hundreds of years. It brings the owners good luck, and by right of possession at the moment you are the owner."

"I still don't want it around."

"OK. We will get rid of it. That's why we are going to New Orleans," I said.

"Why? Are you going to throw it in the Mississippi?"

"No. My cousin in Japan. He's like a spook, but he can't say if he is or isn't, but I know he does a lot of behind the scenes stuff. He has some pretty high-up contacts in the Japanese government. Cousin Rob contacted one of the living heirs of the Tokugawa family, one of the wealthy ones. With his help we've brokered a deal, some Japanese representatives are picking up the sword at the New Orleans airport parking lot."

"Oh hell, here we go again," she said.

"Not this time. The money is in a secured letter of credit. He gets the sword; money goes straight into the bank. No reason for gunplay. My cousin has checked this guy out on a national intelligence level. He's who he says he is."

"How much?"

"Not the 20 million I had hoped," I said. "It's more of a private reward, a finder's fee, than a purchase. It was his family's sword after all."

"OK, how much," Carolyn asked. I ignored the question because we were turning into the parking lot alongside a long black limo with diplomatic plates. "Later," I said. "We have business to transact."

A well-dressed Japanese emerged, bowed as I got out. "You have it?" he asked. I nodded.

"May we examine?"

"Of course," I said, opening the trunk, reaching under the cover that concealed the spare and withdrawing the wood scabbard that protected the blade. He took it carefully and handed it inside the car to two other Japanese wearing white gloves. They carefully withdrew the blade, wiped it down with rice paper, tapped chrysanthemum dust on it, and as one held it the other unrolled a weathered light brown scroll. He held it against the blade, examining close with a magnifying glass. Then came loud jabbering, excited fast talk. I did not need a translator. The Japanese envoys knew they had found the real Honjo.

Just as quickly, they hushed, and from the other side of the car, an elegantly dressed man came around the limo with a formal bearing, approached, and bowed low in a formal bow. I leaned forward slightly in an Americanized bow. He extended his hand. He had tears in his eyes. In halting English he said, "My family thanks you. My country thanks you. The money has been released, please confirm."

I called the bank, where the vice-president of the bank was standing by. "It posted," he said.

I nodded to the Japanese. The first Japanese man approached and the two of them talked back and forth in Japanese. He turned to me. "I must ask one further condition, on your honor, sir?" he said.

"The condition?" I asked.

"When the sword was known, it was easy for a foreign government, your government, to confiscate the sword under your laws imposed on Nippon. We never want to risk that again, so no one must know that the sword has been discovered or returned. It is still lost and will remain lost as far as history is concerned. Is that acceptable?"

"Not only acceptable but preferred," I said. "Although I will have to explain the funds to the tax people in our government."

"No problem," he said. "You were paid for a consultation about swords and collectibles from the Tokugawa family. We will give you a receipt. You might want to come to Japan to make it look better to your government, and we will look at swords and talk about them then," he smiled.

The Japanese speaker glanced over my shoulder at Carolyn in the car, and I watched his face have the typical male reaction to her. I guess I would have to get used to that.

"Your wife?" he asked.

"Soon."

"Very pretty. If you would like to visit Japan our family would be honored to be your host, you can be our guest, perhaps we can have a small ceremony when we restore the sword to its proper stand in our home? Very secure place. Maybe for a honeymoon?"

"That would be nice," I said. "Please let us know a preferred time and we will be there."

"I will. Arrigato." He bowed again.

"You know you can't fly with that on a plane, don't you? I'm sure you do not want to check it."

"Hai. We have a private jet waiting," he explained. "Kugar-san, again, thank you." Again, he bowed. He got back in the car and the others followed. The limo drove away.

Chapter 60

"Are we through with that thing finally," Carolyn asked, still sitting in the car.

"Yes."

"You mean we have finished this easy, after all the difficulties with my brother, all the death, all the lives, it was this easy?"

"Yes." She gave a sigh.

"You didn't ask how much."

"No, I didn't. I don't care, I only wanted it done. Finally. But so many dead. No way it was worth it."

I looked back toward the airport. "You ever tried chargrilled oysters?"

"Never. What are chargrilled oysters?"

"Come on," I said. "We're going to Acme Oyster House. There's one in the airport here."

***

One thing I had come to love about Carolyn is how she enjoys good food. We were on our second dozen chargrilled oysters before she paused to talk.

"How much?"

"Well if we're married, we split it 50-50 right?"

"When we are married there is no 50-50, we both must be all in, we both have 100 percent, you get all of me, I get all of you. We'll be in this thing together. You still want that?" She asked. "Last chance to back out. I will hold you to it."

"I'm still in," I said.

Carolyn paused with a smile, "You know I might be marrying you just to be close to your dog?"

"Street and I come as a set," I said.

"Yes, I want the set, always. I get the dog and all I must do is marry you. Hell of a deal."

***

"OK, there are only two more things I've kept from you if you can stand it," Carolyn said. "Nothing bad, I think, but still may be a shock. Hopefully, neither is a deal breaker. But you still have that option."

"Do you think I can stand it?"

"Not sure you can stand the first one," she said.

"What's the first one?"

"My nickname, the nickname my Grandad gave me. I told you once I would not tell you."

"Yes."

"You are the only person alive that knows this. Everyone called me Carolyn, as long as I can remember. Only my Grandad called me by the name on my birth certificate. My real name is Carol Lynn."

"You are not a Carolyn?" I grinned. "No shit?"

"You OK with that?"

"More than you know." I mumbled, "Not a Carolyn" under my breath. No one at home would believe it.

"OK, one final thing, but it is a biggie."

"Shoot."

"All the times we've done it, all the sex, we've not used anything."

I let that soak in for a second, stunned. "Surely, you're using something, right? You're not on the pill?"

Carolyn shook her head no. "Never was. There was no need, I told you I spent the last year staring out at the ocean. The two guys I dated last year; my dates always used condoms. I guess I got too caught up in the moment with us, too distracted to use common sense."

"What are you saying?"

"At the Walgreens when I went to get the ibuprofen, I bought two EPT tests just to be sure. You know no one will take the results of just one. And the results were the same. You're going to be a daddy. We're pregnant."

The shouts of joy and the dance in the middle of the airport dining area caused the TSA guards to rush us, but once it was all explained we were released with their congratulations to continue our way to the mountains and a new life.

Chapter 61

I was still smiling an hour later as we drove into Mississippi on I-59, just outside Picayune. Carol Lynn was glowing, as only a pregnant woman can.

"In all this other excitement you never said how much reward we got for returning the sword," she asked.

"I will tell you on one condition," I said.

"What is the condition?"

"The baby."

"What about the baby."

"If it is a girl, she can't be named Carolyn."

"With your friend's reactions to the name I wouldn't name a pet skunk Carolyn," she said. "OK, now how much, Daddy?"

"Two million."

"Wow," Carol Lynn said. "Just wow."

"Don't get too excited. We pay taxes and accountants and we have 1.2 mil. We pay off your place and if you want to sell it, figure a wash, maybe 100 grand, pay off my stuff, we are at 1.1. And then there's a ski boat and a pontoon to buy."

"For your grandkids--and kids."

"Yes. Not a time to be chintzy so we're getting close to a mil left."

My cell rang again. "Yes, OK, fine, next week then. And thank you Mr. Patterson. I'll have the papers ready when you get there."

"What was that about?" she asked.

"Oh, I just bought you a wedding present, the Patterson chalet. We're down to 800 grand."

"Think we can get by on that?" she asked, grinning.

"For a while. Trust fund for the kid, and we have a small nest egg and that's about it."

"I guess we have to go to work," she said. "I have an idea though."

"What's that?"

"Real estate."

"Along with everyone else back there?"

"Yes, but I'll look much better on the billboards, and I can sell to men."

"Oh, I'm sure you can," I laughed. "You know that could work. I can sell because I think the clients might catch on to my expressing my love for the place, they might feel it and catch it too."

"With the two us working clients together, they wouldn't stand a chance, would they?" she said.

"And what would we call our new agency? "Madison and Madison?" "Mr. & Mrs. Kugar Realty?"

"No, I have the name too," she said. "The logo will be a chess piece. We'll call it 'White Knight Realty'." She laughed at my sideways glance. "I love you," she said, and she didn't say it like an actress.

Carolyn snuggled under my arm, turned on Pandora, and damned if it wasn't a Journey song only this time a different lyric stuck became the ear worm in my head: "It goes on and on and on and on."

THE END

#